the turning

WHAT CURIOSITY KILLS

helen ellis

sourcebooks
fire

YA
ELL

Sourcebooks and the colophon are registered trademarks of
Sourcebooks, Inc.

Published by Sourcebooks Fire, an imprint of Sourcebooks, Inc.
P.O. Box 4410, Naperville, Illinois 60567-4410
(630) 961-3900
Fax: (630) 961-2168
teenfire.sourcebooks.com

Library of Congress Cataloging-in-Publication data is on file with the
publisher.

Printed and bound in the United States of America.
SB 10 9 8 7 6 5 4 3 2 1

12/10 - B&T - $14.99

For Lex Haris,
Greek god among men

She turns herself round and she smiles and she says,
"This is it, that's the end of the joke"

—The Psychedelic Furs, "Pretty in Pink"

What happens is...

I want to scream for help, but pain that feels like fire ants has found me. The ants crawl up and out of my knee socks and take over every bit of my flesh. They are between my toes, behind my ears, and in every crevice in between. They scamper across my scalp. They bite. Their bites are unbearable. I twist and scratch within the suffocating comforter. I'm trapped.

The boys lean over me, say things—to me, to each other—I can't make out. My hearing is fading. I'm shrinking. The boys' faces get bigger and rise like moons. One of them blinks. When his eyes close, they are chestnut. Open, they are emerald green. He smiles, parts his teeth, and unrolls a long, narrow pink tongue. He licks the tips of his incisors, which have grown past his lower gums to form fine points.

He purrs, his voice velvet. He says, "Don't worry, Kitty. There are no such things as vampires."

What happened was...

chapter one

I knew something was wrong with me when I fell asleep in school. I never fall asleep in public because it is way too embarrassing. Your face goes slack. If you're sitting up straight, your mouth hangs open. You could say something stupid or say someone's name or make some weird, inappropriate noise. You could snore. Twitch. Drool! In the movies, people watch other people sleep and say that it's beautiful. Those people are crazy—or in love. Trust me. Nobody at Purser-Lilley Academy loves me that much.

What I did was roll out of the seal position and crash on my Pilates mat. The seal is when you start on your back with your hands clutching your ankles and your knees bent out to the sides, making your legs look like a diamond. You're supposed to clap the soles of your feet three times and then rock forward onto your butt and clap your feet three times again. Then, roll back and forth, clapping like a maniac—*Ar! Ar! Ar!*—until you build up enough momentum to throw yourself forward into a standing position. You're supposed to end up with hands in the air like a gymnast.

I ended up in the fetal position. For five full un-revivable minutes.

My friend Marjorie says I was motionless for so long, she thought I was dead. Marjorie's sister promises me that the rumors I was sucking my thumb are untrue. *My* sister will tell anyone she hears spreading lies about me that my hands were curled up under my chin.

"Like she was all Laura Ingalls and shit, tying a bonnet," my sister says.

You might wonder how my best friend, her sister, my sister, and I are in the same tenth-grade gym class; how my sister can curse in front of teachers and get away with it; how a high school gets twenty Pilates mats and towers drilled into what was once a basketball court. The answer to all these questions is: money.

Marjorie and her sister Magnolia—nicknamed Mags—are in vitro twins. Sometimes, we call them Baby A and Baby B, which is what they went by before they were born and their parents "deselected" the weaker of the quads, C and D. Kathryn Ann wanted to experience the blessing of childbirth, but not *that* much of a blessing. She didn't want to be bedridden. She wanted to get back to her call-in cable TV talk show, *Chime In with Kathryn Ann.* A former district attorney, Kathryn Ann had made her name by charging drunk drivers with murder and now makes a living pressuring upstanding citizens to go after drunks and pedophiles and anyone else who, as she says, *could be shot for less.*

Kathryn Ann was forty-four when she had Marjorie and

Mags. Long story short: She built herself a career and then remembered she wanted kids. But her ovaries were like, *What?*

Kathryn Ann wrote a check to her fertility specialist. And then another. As did a lot of older couples who wanted kids late in life and found themselves "reproductively challenged." At Purser-Lilley, there are fourteen sets of twins and six sets of triplets.

We also have a bunch of kids who don't look like their folks. You can spot adopted kids because most Upper East Side parents go for Asians. An Asian baby says you have twenty thousand dollars, plus cash to fly to the other side of the world and put yourself up in a hotel for two weeks. Asian babies are also good because their biological parents aren't going to show up to reclaim them. At Purser-Lilley, there are four Korean boys and eight Chinese girls. One of them, Ling Ling Lebowitz, is the meanest girl I've ever met.

Ling Ling likes to tell me that I am white trash. I don't think anybody uses this term anymore, but she read *Gone with the Wind* and fell in love with the slur. She says, "One day, your real parents are going to kidnap you and hold you for ransom. They're gonna take you back to Ala-*bama*. Say good-bye, 72nd and Lex! Good-bye, Bravo marathons! Your real parents are so poor, all you'll have to do for fun is fish for *crawdaddies* in the *crick!*"

My response to Ling Ling's barbs (another beaut is, "You're so flat-chested, your redneck mama must have breast-fed you

Mountain Dew!") is: "Could be." This stumps her and shuts her up, but the next time I run into her, she's prepared with another verbal assault. I don't enjoy it, but I bear it and say "Could be," and it's over in a minute. I'm not going to argue with her. That will prolong her abuse. Besides, most of what she makes up is actually true: the poor part, the Alabama part—but not the part about rednecks plotting to kidnap me.

As far as adoption goes, my sister and I are an oddity at Purser-Lilley because we came from within the United States, and our folks didn't get us when they were middle-aged and we were infants. When they decided to start a family, they cast their nets wide and took the first kids they caught: me from Alabama, Octavia from Nebraska. Unlike Ling Ling, my sister and I have memories of our eight years before our adoptive parents saved us—memories we do our best to forget.

My birth parents were neglectful. I spent a lot of time alone. I barely went to school. I survived by eating so much generic cereal out of the box that to this day, I won't walk down the breakfast aisle at Gristedes. When a social worker came and got me, my biological parents missed every court date to get me back. If it weren't for my southern accent—which I *cain't* shake to save my life—I might have been able to blend in at Purser-Lilley. My same-age sister's appearance stopped any chance of that.

Octavia is the only student in the whole school who's black—or, as Purser-Lilley mandates we say, *African American*. Her minority status was our ticket into private school. Over frozen hot chocolates at Serendipity 3, when Octavia and I were both thirteen, Dad had a brain freeze. He let it slip that success can often be attributed to what you look like. To this day, my sister's greatest discovery is the race card.

The thing is, she taught herself to keep it real from TV Land reruns of shows older than we are, so *227*, *Living Single*, and *Martin* are her guides. Our parents ignore her *Yo*'s and *It's like dis and like dat*'s and when she goes, "Can I *ax* you a question?" because Octavia makes all As, and Mom says trying new identities is part of growing up. Mom says when she was our age, she imitated California girls and said *Totally!* when she agreed with you, and when she didn't, *Gag me with a spoon*.

In school, Octavia gets away with murder. If she doesn't want to be called on, she folds her arms across her chest and gives the teacher a look that says, *Are you calling on me 'cause I'm black?* If she wants an extra brownie at lunch, she says to the Jamaican lunch lady, "Hook a sistah up!" If she doesn't want to play basketball, she says, "What, Coach, you think I was *born* to shoot hoops?"

That's how we ended up with just half a basketball court for dribble drills and H-O-R-S-E. Our last coach told Octavia (in front a bunch of us) that the only reason she got into Purser-Lilley was to help us win the city title. Other parents were so afraid of being labeled racists that they withheld their second-semester tuition checks until the principal eliminated competitive sports.

Which brings us back to yours truly being all *Little House on the Prairie* on a Pilates mat.

• • •

At lunch, Ling Ling stops by my table and offers me a baby bottle she snuck from Health and Development. Ha, ha. Very funny. I sucked my thumb, so I'm a baby.

My sister comes up behind Ling Ling and pokes her shoulder hard. Octavia warns, "You better check yo self before you wreck yo self."

Ling Ling doesn't test her. She scuttles off, prop slipped into her book bag, because she wants nothing to do with my sister. Ling Ling teased Octavia *once* about domestic adoption and was met with a brutally honest tirade about birth parents mutilated by farm equipment; the greedy, heinous devil that is America's health-insurance system; an older brother jailed; a sister pregnant and married at sixteen; another sister missing; and four years of personal foster-care horror stories. Octavia put an end to any and all future Ling Ling harassment with: "Uh, and if you don't know, now you know!"

Octavia plops down next to me with a brownie the size of two fists. Across from us sit Marjorie and Mags, who are the same shade of pale from their platinum-blond heads to their never-painted toenails (unlike Kathryn Ann, who will not be seen without blood-red tips and lips and a permanent spray tan). Ling Ling calls the twins albinos every chance she gets. Her favorite zinger is that they might have had a little color if their mom had let them cook as directed and not scheduled her C-section a month early to coincide with the verdict of a trial she was covering.

With Ling Ling out of earshot, I ask the group, "Did I really look like a baby?"

Marjorie says, "A dead baby. I kept shaking you. I thought you'd never wake up. I nearly cried."

I gush, "Aww."

Mags says, "It wasn't *Aww*. It was scary—but you definitely weren't sucking your thumb."

The twins look at each other. They are mentally conferring. Eyebrows arch. Lips twist. Noses scrunch in concentrated worry. It drives me nuts when they do this, but I've known them long enough to read a line or two from their minds.

"What are you deciding to tell or not tell me?"

The twins swing around to Octavia, the official teller of all you might not want to know but should know.

"What?" I plead. "Okay, don't tell me. No, tell me!"

My sister leans into me and whispers without covering her mouth, "Shaniqua…"

(My real name is Mary, which I hate. What's worse is that when I took my adoptive parents' last name, Richards, I was branded with the 1970s TV alter ego of Mary Tyler Moore—a grinning, mousy-haired, perpetually single brunette. My parents say I can legally change my first name when I find one I like better—which I never do—but Octavia's always offering suggestions).

She whispers, "It was weird. I've slept in the same room with you for years and never seen you do this. Or *heard* you, is more like it. And to tell you the truth—no offense—I don't want to ever hear you do it again. It's not a sound I want to wake up to, trapped in a dark room with you, in the middle of the night. Now, get a hold of yourself. Chill. With the three of us around, Ling Ling wasn't close enough to pick up on it. But we did."

The twins nod. Then, their bobbleheads stop. They pick up their ginkgo frappuccinos, made exclusively by Purser-Lilley's Starbucks, and each take a sip. The drinks stop halfway up their straws as they anticipate what my sister says next.

"Girl, you was purring!"

chapter two

At home, my family sits down to dinner. House rule is that we eat together five nights a week. If somebody has something to do at seven thirty, we eat at six. If my dad stays late at the office, we eat when he comes home. No TV trays, no restaurants. Sometimes, we order in, but then we eat at the table off proper plates, not off paper or out of cool, origami-looking Chinese cartons (which in Manhattan exist only on TV).

Tonight's topic: no more cell phones and no computers in our room.

Mom says, "You girls are wired. In all senses of the word. It's like a constant feed of M&M's. Your every thought, every mundane action, has to be communicated like it's life or death. *I'm on the bus. I'm at the movies.* You can't think for yourselves. *What time does the movie start? Where's the nearest Starbucks? Should I get a tall latte or an* iced *tall latte?* You check your messages every ten seconds to see if your friends need answers. *What's up? Nothing, what's up with you? You*, mind you, spelled with one letter, *U*. It used to be there was one idiot box. Now they come in all shapes and sizes. You're over stimulated. That's why you're falling asleep in school."

"I fell asleep once," I protest.

Dad says, "Once is enough."

It's hard to argue with them about cell phones. My parents don't use them. They're Luddites. Well, they're Luddites in the way that Marjorie and Mags are albinos. To Mom and Dad, old phones are art. The one in their bedroom is a five-pound, black-metal rotary. The kitchen phone is a wall-mounted, yellow, push-button number straight out of *Freaky Friday*—the original with Jodie Foster, field hockey, and orthodontia that could be from *Saw*.

BlackBerries, iPhones, and all the rest were banned from Purser-Lilley last year because it was electronic note-passing bedlam; our collective grade average dropped, and the requisite five percent of seniors did not get into Harvard. Teachers thought we had brain cancer. Tumors were the new Uggs. Now you're allowed to use cell phones on the street outside the school, but once you pass through the front gates, you might as well carry a grenade in your uniform blazer. Per an official addendum to the Purser-Lilley Code of Conduct: you don't snooze it, you lose it.

Confiscated cells have been passed around the teachers' lounge for laughs, I'm sure of it. Ling Ling's sweet sixteen was canceled because of phone calls made to her Park Avenue apartment from Scared Straight, Planned Parenthood, and the U.S. Army recruitment office, which her mom refused to believe were phony. I'm almost positive the callers were Ms. Lawrence and Mr. Marks (feminist literature and trig). When we were freshmen,

Ling Ling got the whole school to nickname them Fatty Cakes and McLovin.

Octavia tries arguing about cells with Mom anyway. My sister is the youngest-ever captain of the Purser-Lilley debate team, which has been undefeated two years running. I once asked her, just to get a rise out of her: "Do you feel you have to work twice as hard to do as well as you do because you're a minority?"

She said, "No, Eudora, I'm just smart."

Now she says, "Mom, it's unsafe not having a cell. What if something bad happens?"

"Then, something bad happens. We'll find out eventually."

"Like we did with your sister's narcolepsy," jokes Dad.

Octavia groans. "But *I* didn't fall asleep. It was Enya—"

"Mary," Mom corrects her.

"*Mary*, not me. Why should I be punished?"

"Believe it or not, your mother and I don't think that we're punishing you. You'll sleep better and go to sleep sooner. Worst-case scenario, you'll do what we did at your age and read in bed with a flashlight."

"Did you really do that?" I ask. Octavia smirks.

"No," Dad confesses. "I had a TV in my room."

Mom says, "And that's why his grades were so bad."

"Hey, are you forgetting I skipped the fourth grade?" Dad asks.

"*After* the fourth grade, your grades were terrible." Mom rolls her eyes. "Have *you* forgotten that your shrink attributes all your issues to skipping?"

"What issues? I don't have any issues." Dad often plays dumb.

Octavia says, "What does this have to do with anything? We don't have a TV in our room."

Our family has one TV. (Luddites, remember?) It's in the living room. If you're watching, everyone else is watching with you, or they know what's on. And—wait for it—we don't own a DVD player. It's not because my parents are seriously anti-technology or that my sister and I are overprotected. My parents just hate extra stuff. Mom's mantra is: *We are not hoarders.* Every year, we give away clothes we've outgrown (or we're too old for), books we've read (or are never going to get to), and extras ("Tell me," says Mom, "do we really need *two* garlic presses?"). Dad can't be convinced Netflix is necessary when we get all the movie channels. Having never had more than one TV, this isn't a hardship. Octavia and I don't miss out on much—unless you call *much* vegging out on the sofa and watching *Twilight* eight times in a row.

Our folks DVR their old favorites for us. With my dad, it's *The Warriors* and *The Taking of Pelham 123*—1970s movies that represent the New York he grew up in; where subways were graffitied, everybody had a switchblade, and after eleven, you could get yourself killed. Mom goes for all things teenage-angst. She got weepy when John Hughes passed away and then nearly keeled over herself when she found out Marjorie and Mags hadn't seen the Molly Ringwald trifecta (*Sixteen Candles*, *The Breakfast Club*, and *Pretty in Pink*). Mom wanted to watch them with us, but Dad dragged her out for Ben & Jerry's because she was reciting every line.

"'I can't believe this. They fucking forgot my birthday.'"

"Yes, dear," said Dad. "John Hughes was your George Lucas."

Octavia and I tried to get into the original *Star Wars* trilogy for Dad but couldn't. *Luke, I am your father!* Well, duh. Who didn't see that coming? Dad and every other *Dungeons & Dragons* fanatic apparently. Dad shrugged off how jaded we were, but he still keeps a lightsaber on the top shelf of his closet, and on Halloween, he makes Mom wear earmuffs that look like hair cinnamon rolls.

Mom says to Octavia, "You may not have a TV in your room, but you have YouTube, Facebook, Twitter, and all that other garbage on your computer that keeps—"

"my mind on my money and my money on my mind!"

"—that keeps you quoting Snoop Dogg instead of Shakespeare."

Dad grins at Mom. "Since when do you quote Shakespeare?"

"'Tis a nobler…'tis a far, far better…" She laughs. "Oh, you know what I mean! From now on, girls, your laptops stay out in the open and go off at eight o'clock. Mary, you'll work in the kitchen. Octavia, you'll work on the dining room table."

The dining room table is in the living room because we don't have a room especially for eating. Yes, this is the Upper East Side, but Anderson Cooper's mom is not our mom. My parents have plenty of money in the grand scheme of things—they can pay our tuition, send us to college, take us on vacation, buy us nice clothes—but they don't have the kind of New York City wealth that takes three or four generations to squander. If we swapped moms with Marjorie and Mags, we'd have our own Vanderbilt-like bedrooms and adjoining bathroom, plus a library and a study. I've never understood the difference between those—except that one has leather couches, which the twins' cats have scratched up and which Octavia refuses to sit on because the claw marks give her the creeps. But I digress. Life isn't a Disney movie where you wake up in somebody else's body and realize you were happy just the way you were. Besides, Octavia and I would never swap moms with anyone.

● ● ●

After eight, my laptop is closed. Mom has put a plate of homemade chocolate chip cookies on top to seal the deal. I have to get through four chapters of *A Tale of Two Cities*. Octavia is done with her homework. She's always done first. She's watching TV with my parents in the living room on the other side of the kitchen wall. As a reward for a job well done, she has clicker control. It's a Tuesday night in January. For the next two hours, I'm going to overhear auditions for *American Idol*.

I hate the show, but Octavia loves it. She's always trying to convince me to give it another shot. It's the debater in her. She tries to convince me I should change my mind about everything. The situation in Afghanistan is worse than the situation in Iraq. September 11 was an inside job. Health care should never be free. A woman's right to choose is wiggida wiggida wiggida whack. Arguing is a game to her. She picks pro or con and runs with it until her opponent is too exhausted to catch up. I'm not sure she loves *American Idol* as much as she says she does, but she puts up a heck of a fight.

Sample debate:

Octavia: "It's all about second chances for girls like Kelly."

Me: "Clarkson or Pickler?"

Octavia: "Either. Those girls are one in the same."

Me: "One's rock, one's country."

Octavia: "My point is that those girls come from Podunk, U.S.A. Humble beginnings. Without *American Idol*, they'd never be more than cashiers who can carry a tune. Not one overprivileged kid ever makes it to the finals. *American Idol* loves oil-rig workers and teenage moms and ROTC kids back from the war. Girls like Kelly are taken out of hopeless situations and given a future with financial security. Like us. How can you turn your nose up at a genie-in-a-bottle show when our parents are the real-life Simon and Paula!"

Me: "You mean Simon and Ellen."

My sister rolls her eyes at my nitpicking. She knows how to go for the jugular and she got me. She was right, but what I said at the time was: "Could be."

I open the paperback with the guillotine on the cover and read, *It was the best of times, it was the worst of times.*

Simon's English accent interrupts from the TV. "You have a voice that would make an angel's ears bleed."

"Turn it down please!" I holler.

Simon Cowell is the rest of the world's Ling Ling Lebowitz.

I reach for a cookie. Take a bite. The chocolate melts on my tongue while the cookie part sticks to the roof of my mouth. It is perfect. But I can't bring myself to chew. There is nothing wrong with the cookie. It's delicious. The warm, half-moon remainder smells sweet, but all I want to do—as Octavia would so eloquently put it—is drop it like it's hot.

The severed edge of the cookie crumbles when it lands on the table. The crumbs glisten because they are wet.

I am salivating. The bite in my mouth dissolves with no help from my teeth. I am desperately thirsty. My mind gets a picture in it; an ad from a grocery-store circular. Not for Coke, not for seltzer, not for Snapple. For milk.

I have to have it, and I have to have it right now.

I push back the metal-framed chair, and it scrapes like bad brakes.

"Turn it down yourself!" yells Octavia.

Simon Cowell says, "That wasn't singing, sweetheart."

With two steps, I am at the fridge. My hand is on the handle. I swing it open with so much force, it swings back. The door smacks the rubber sealant and makes a sound that Jim Carrey makes in most of his movies. I steady myself. My thirst is so overpowering, my hands shake. I reach out and take the handle gingerly this time.

Open...

With both hands, I grip a two-liter carton of whole milk. The carton slips from my hands. The milk spurts onto the floor.

I cry over it. Yes, I am crying over spilled milk. This realization doesn't make me laugh; it makes me sob harder. Crying is another thing I hate to do where other people might see me. When I cry, I turn ugly and get loud. But I can't stop myself. I'm so thirsty! All I wanted was some milk! I kneel to see if any of it is salvageable.

"Mary!" Mom shouts like I'm not right in front of her. She shouts my name over and over like I'm deaf and miles away.

I don't respond. Cast in the light of the open refrigerator, I know what I'm doing is wrong. It is vile. But the milk is so creamy. I've never tasted such cold creaminess before. Suddenly, I'm dirt poor again, and the milk is liquid gold. I'm on *American Idol*, and the milk will turn me into Carrie Underwood. *Jesus, take the wheel!* With a lick, I'm addicted. But I convulse at the competing flavor of a terra-cotta floor tile, which hasn't been mopped in a week, against my tongue.

chapter three

Heroin," Dad pronounces once they've wrestled me off my hands and knees. "You fall asleep in the middle of the day and eat off the floor when you're on heroin."

Octavia says, "She's not on heroin."

"Well, grass doesn't do that."

Octavia shakes her head. "Dad, nobody says *grass*."

Mom's never been one of those parents who, when they come in from outside, wash their hands before they hug you. She doesn't like clutter, but she's not a neat freak either. Right now, she's standing sock-footed in spilled milk. Her hand hasn't left my forehead.

"She's burning up, Scott. She has a fever."

Without another word, Dad scoops me up, all fire and rescue. I hear him stifle a groan from my weight. I'm not heavy, but I'm not a little kid anymore. The first time he carried me was when he taught me to ride a bike in Central Park. My front tire hit a crack, and I flipped over the handlebars. He left the bike there and carried me all the way home. We never saw that bike again, and my parents swore they didn't care. In all my life, I'd never felt so loved. For the next year or so,

I walked into walls, shut my fingers in doors, and chewed too fast so that I'd bite the inside of my mouth to test that their love wasn't fleeting. Every time I cried out in pain, Dad scooped me up and whisked me to safety. A cure was always in their medicine cabinet.

Dad sits me down on the closed toilet in their bathroom. He's the managing editor of a financial news website, so he's no tough guy, but he keeps his cool in the face of a skinned knee, a nose bleed—or, in this case, a fever of a 102.

"Scott, should I call 911?" Mom asks anxiously from the doorway.

"Calling 911 is going to land her in the emergency room. We'll be there all night, and she'll catch something worse. Give her four Tylenol and get her into a lukewarm tub. If the fever doesn't break by midnight, *then* we'll take her to Lenox Hill."

Dad leaves to clean up the kitchen. I'm weak, so I let Mom draw my bath and Octavia hold a Dixie cup to my lips as I swallow each extra-strength caplet. When the tub's full, I wave them away.

Mom says, "I'll be right outside."

Octavia goes with her. I imagine my sister plants herself back in front of the TV, but I know Mom's ear is pressed against the bathroom door, eavesdropping for the slightest sound of distress.

I take my time peeling off each sock. I unzip my jeans. To slip out of them, I ease down onto the black-and-white checkerboard tiled floor, so if I get dizzy, I won't fall off the toilet and crack my skull. I shimmy out, and the tiles are cool against my bare legs, which feel as fevered as my face. Off comes my Nada Surf hoodie. All that's left on me is my pitiful A-cup padded bra and Victoria's Secret boyshort panties that read *I ♥ Geeks.*

Mom calls, "Are you in the tub yet? Do you need help?"

"No," I manage. "I'm fine."

Mom hasn't heard the bathwater splash. If I don't make some noise that shows progress, she'll be in here, and I'll be mortified. Sleeping, crying, licking milk off the floor—I'm not about to add public nakedness to my growing list of humiliations. I prop myself up on my elbows and glare at the small black radiator that hisses to life.

Mom hears it too. "Do you want me to turn that off for you, baby?"

"No, thanks."

Most everyone in our co-op is in for the night, so the super has cranked up the heat. All over the apartment, I hear the iron beasts clank, spit, and roar. To turn the blistering on/off nozzle righty-tighty, I use my sweatshirt as an oven mitt. Even with the valve shut, the radiator ribs will remain hot and turn this bathroom into a sauna.

I brace myself along the long side of the tub. I've sweat through my underwear. My hair sticks to the back of my neck. I'm trembling, but the thought of getting into the tub makes me cringe. The water is a sheet of glass. If I touch it, it will shatter. Then, I'll be in worse pain.

"Baby, are you all right?"

"Yes," I lie.

I have to do something or Mom's going to come in here. The only thing that sounds good to me is sleep. That milk was a sedative. I fight the urge to lie back down. Maybe if I stir the water around, Mom will believe I've done what she wanted and I can go to bed. I reach my hand into the tub to test the temperature.

"Good girl!" Mom thinks the splash was my foot.

I jerk my hand out, and Mom claps because she thinks it's my other foot going under the surface.

I shake the water off, and it splashes the shower curtain, which has sailboats on it so the bathroom isn't too frilly for my dad. The water is slimy like the inside of a sink pipe when you stick your finger down it to fish out a ring. To placate my mom, I stir the water with the plunger.

Mom calls, "Cool off. I'll come back in a little while with the thermometer." Her footsteps fade, and I wonder why she's not worried that I'll pass out and drown.

Outside the bathroom window, kids are yammering and smoking while waiting for the Crosstown 72. Our apartment is on the second floor above the bus stop. I can hear entire conversations, and while I'm not a smoker myself, I can smell the difference between Marlboros and American Spirits. This is a prewar building from 1917. Even with the windows shut, everything gets in, including a draft.

I rest the side of my head against the blinds. It's less than 30 degrees outside. The icy air seeps through the window. I'm covered in goose bumps. I unhook my dad's terry-cloth robe from the back of the door. The robe is heavy. My knees buckle. I steady myself and then part the blinds and peer out.

The neon lights of the bus stop glow in the dark. The kids, four boys and a girl, are talking about—what else?—how cold January is. The boys are bundled in what never goes out of style in Manhattan: black down jackets that make them look like charred Michelin Men. I'm sure that three of them don't go to my school because their haircuts would never fly. Too cool for wool caps, one kid's hair is spiked with Elmer's Glue, another's is dirtied into blond dreadlocks, and a third's is shaved to reveal a scalp tattoo.

The remaining boy better fits the Purser-Lilley mold, except for the cheap black-and-gray-checked scarf wrapped around his nose and mouth. By the way that he tugs at it, I can tell it itches and ain't Barney's cashmere.

The boys might be my age, might be older. I think everyone in high school looks older than me. Every time I look (or don't look) in the mirror, I feel like I'm twelve. Mom says she forever feels sixteen. I don't know who I feel sorrier for.

The girl wears a white version of the Michelin Man jacket. The hood is trimmed with rabbit fur. The drawstrings end in fuzzy rabbit balls. I've seen it on skinny Purser-Lilley moms; it seems too expensive for this crowd. The girl throws her head back and laughs.

My eyes widen. *Hello, Ling Ling Lebowitz.*

Ling Ling, a tiny girl who is always cold, is warmed by the group. She slips in and out of their spooning embraces. She's a dodge ball that's not thrown but gently passed from one easy catch to the next. The boys encircle her and take turns getting cozy. If Octavia saw this, she'd call Ling Ling a *ho.* But Ling Ling doesn't look ho-ish. She looks perfectly at ease. I'm jealous. No boy has ever wrapped his arms around me, let alone four at once.

The bus arrives, and the group piles on. Ling Ling chooses a window seat. The boys elbow each other over who's going to sit beside her because they can't pass her around on the bus. The driver closes the doors, and the bus rocks from the suction. The boys stretch out their arms and pretend to be surfing.

Ling Ling snatches the tail end of that one boy's cheap checked scarf. The boy tips toward her, bats her hand away, frees himself. Fringe comes off in her mitten. Ling Ling grabs another handful, higher up at his throat. The scarf tightens around his nose and mouth. His forehead turns red. Does she want to borrow the scarf or cut off the blood to his brain?

The other boys prod him. Ling Ling has chosen him; he should sit his ass down. He settles in beside her and loosens his scarf but doesn't remove it. He takes his cap off, and out pops a cloud of black curly hair. He turns toward Ling Ling, leans into her, and whispers I don't know what. But I see who he is.

Nick Martin.

The one Purser-Lilley boy who is not too skinny and not at all fat. He's not too tall and not shorter than me. He has dark brown eyes and what looks like a year-round tan. Every summer, he disappears from Manhattan and goes to Athens and the Greek islands to spend three months with his grandparents. Every first day of school, he smells like the beach.

Do I need to mention that Nick Martin is my not-so-secret crush? With that description, what else could he be?

The bus veers into traffic, and Nick looks over his shoulder in my direction as if he's forgetting something. That I live here? That instead of being the tablespoon in Ling Ling's measuring set of boys, he'd meant to acknowledge me for the first time in our lives? He keeps his gaze in line with mine. The bathroom blinds are closed, but I get a weird sensation that we're making eye contact. I feel something between us—something warm and incredibly real.

I put my hand over my drumming heart. Like the bus, Nick is now long gone, but I feel like he's still out there. Closer than before…getting closer…about to ask my doorman to give me a buzz. It's ridiculous, *I'm* ridiculous, but I take another peek. For what? His bus dust?

What I find is a cat.

Sitting on top of the bus stop is the strangest cat I've ever seen. It's not six-toed or deformed in any way. It's a calico, but its markings make it look like it's wearing a mask. The rest of its face is copper, except for a patch on its mouth that looks like zinc oxide. It has long black whiskers. Its eyes are emerald green.

The thing is big. And this big thing is looking right at me.

Except for deli cats, you never see strays in Manhattan. Health inspectors fine delis $400 the first time they find a cat, then $1,000 the next. Owners won't get rid of them because cats keep out rats, and rats will shut a place down. Deli cats are obese and dirty from sleeping on floors covered in filth from constant streams of customers. Octavia won't go into delis because she swears she can smell cat piss over burnt coffee, open vats of creamed soup, stale mops, and even sponges. Plus, she's scared of a paw coming out from under somewhere and taking a swipe at her shoelaces. Often, you see a pair of eyes blink at you from behind the potato chip rack. I recognize these emerald eyes from the deli, right around the corner.

What these eyes are saying to me is: *Open your window, and let me spring in.*

There is a knock on the bathroom door.

When I don't answer right away, Mom turns the handle. Her face melts in relief. She's happy to see me on my feet and in Dad's robe. She thinks I did my time in the tub and felt well enough to get out and get dressed. Slipping the digital thermometer under my tongue, she steers me to sit down. She sweeps my clothes into a messy bunch under one arm and drains the water by pulling the plug. She's out and back from the hamper before the thermometer beeps. She reads it. More relief.

"Ninety-nine point nine. This must one of those twenty-four-hour bugs. Twelve hours maybe. Thank God for small miracles."

chapter four

In bed, I'm too hot to get entirely under the covers. I start with one leg out and then stick both legs out so I'm wearing a loincloth. Then, I'm on top of the duvet. I push and pull at it with my feet and hands until I've made a feathery nest. I'm not interested in my pillow. I kick it off my top bunk onto the floor.

"Stop squirming!" Octavia scoots out from her bottom bunk. She picks up the pillow and swings it military, soap-in-a-sock style across my side.

"Oof! Quit it! Leave me alone."

"Leave *me* alone," Octavia says. "You're like a wrestler up there. How many body-slams does it take for you to go to sleep?"

"Girls…"

My dad's voice is right outside our closed bedroom door. He's in the kitchen, and we're getting too loud. *Riled up* is what he calls it. We have to calm down. It's a school night. There is nothing my parents value more than a good night's sleep. *Girls…* used to be followed by *don't make me come in there*, but in all these years, he's never come in.

My folks dread a rebellious phase, but they should know

that such a phase will never come. When you've lived the lives Octavia and I lived before we were adopted, you've been punished enough. Nowadays, you do what you're told. You are grateful for parents who love you (or even tough-love you). You are grateful for corny TV shows, for a roof over your head, and beds—even if those beds are bunk beds and y'all are sixteen.

My sister whispers, "Go to sleep, and cover your face with your pillow. I've got a debate against Nightingale tomorrow, and I am *not* catching your germs."

"I'm not sick."

"Okay, Britney, then you are delusional."

"Am not."

"You have a fever."

"Do not! I'm just warm. Like I've got a mohair sweater on and can't take it off."

Octavia says, "Thanks so much for the gory details. The flu is all I need tomorrow when I argue whether Harry Potter is a threat to Christianity."

"You're not going to catch anything! There's nothing to catch."

"How do you know?"

"I don't know. I just *know*. It's like a lisp. You can't catch a lisp."

Octavia laughs. "People pick up other people's accents all the time. You go all backwoods when you talk to Kathryn Ann."

"Kathryn Ann's from Mississippi, not Alabama."

"Southern is Southern."

"This ain't a debate."

"See, there's that accent. You get angry, out it cuh-*hums*."

See? Jugular. I try: "Maybe I've got allergies. You can't catch allergies."

"You don't have allergies." Octavia insists. "You'd be sneezing or breaking out in hives or your throat would close up. Allergies are all about dying or phlegm. Besides, you've never had them. What crossed your path in the last twenty-four hours that's never crossed it before?"

Other than the deli cat, I can't think of anything. Like the rest of my sister's opponents (no matter what color their cardigans), I roll over and concede.

●　●　●

I wake up at 3:00 a.m. I don't have to pee. I didn't have a bad dream. I'm not hot. I haven't gotten too cold. I am simply wide awake in what is officially the middle of the night. It is dead quiet.

Unlike every other room in our apartment, ours is the only one that faces the courtyard—which isn't a courtyard, really, but the back service area. Instead of a metal fire escape, you step out of our windows onto an 8-by-14-foot cement landing. The landing connects to a long, unsafe row of cast iron steps that lead down to a cement pit bordered by tall brick walls. Over those walls are B-sides of four three-story town houses.

When our second-floor neighbor gets off the elevator with her five Shih Tzus, you can hear them yipping from our living room. In my parents' room, you hear our aging upstairs neighbor's TV when she falls asleep. Mom and Dad wake up having learned odd facts by osmosis about catfish noodling and 198-pound tumors with teeth. In our kitchen, for two hours every afternoon, you hear our second-floor opera-singer neighbor practice her scales. Scales are not *La Traviata*. Scales are shorthand for shrieking. When Octavia and I moved in, we thought this place was haunted.

But in our room, you rarely hear anything other than rain against the metal air-conditioning unit. About four times a year, we hear a doorman sweep stuff off the landing. You'd be amazed at what the so-called Upper East Side elite toss out their windows for fear of discovery: cigarettes and condoms.

The only other time anyone else is back there is when the exterminator comes to clear the rat traps. No building exists without vermin in this city. Mice and rats don't care if you reside squarely in the center of the 10021 zip code. If there is a way in, they will get in. Once, we caught a mouse that had eaten a hole through a Wonder Bread bag on our kitchen countertop. When we found its chewed entryway around the dishwasher drain pipe and stuffed a Brillo pad into it, my dad said to us girls, "Don't look so relieved. Where there's one, there's a hundred."

I imagine a charcoal-gray blanket of them on the landing,

lying side by side by side, head to tail to head to tail to head to tail. The blanket moves with their combined tiny breaths. Their backs ripple like lake water in the night.

Okay, I've scared myself into having to pee.

I ease down from my top bunk so as not to wake Octavia, who's a light sleeper. She keeps a wool throw tucked under my mattress so it hangs down and curtains her bottom bunk like a train's sleeping compartment. Eight years ago, she originally asked for the blanket to muffle my tossing and turning, but I think she wanted to hide how scared she was of sleeping in a new place with new parents and, underneath me a new sister. Now, the blanket provides her with privacy. The curtained bunk is her very own studio apartment. She reads in there and talks on the phone in there. She gets dressed and undressed in there too. Despite her bravado, she's bizarrely shy about her body. In all our years together, I've never seen her fully naked. I don't know what she thinks she's got that I don't.

Octavia shouts: "Witch!"

My flesh goes goose for the second time tonight. Then, I realize my sister is debating in her sleep. She does it before every match. When her topic was assisted suicide, all night long she shouted, "Syringe!" My guess is that she's hoping she wins the coin flip tomorrow so she can argue that Harry Potter is indeed a threat to all things holy and call J. K. Rowling a witch. When debating, Octavia has much more fun bible-thumping on the overzealous religious right.

I creep across the carpet. Windows are on one side of the room; desks line the opposite wall. Our shared bathroom is half the size of our parents'. I shut the door and take two steps to the toilet and then sit down with my back to the bathroom window, which also overlooks the landing. In the darkness and solitude, I remember the blanket of mice.

I drop my face into my hands. I'm getting myself worked up over nothing. I don't have a fever anymore. At least, I don't feel as if I do. Dang it, I'm not afraid—of anything or anyone. To prove it, I dare myself to wake up Octavia. I pee without putting toilet paper on top of the water to soundproof the stream. I flush instead of letting the yellow mellow until it's time to rise and shine. Emboldened, I stand up, face the window, and yank the cord to the blinds.

It takes a few seconds for my vision to adjust, but then I see them.

Mice.

A blanket of them, just as I'd imagined.

They whip their triangular heads in my direction. I draw in a deep breath to scream, but they scatter before I exhale. They are liquid-fast—a lawn sprinkler turned on full blast. They filter into building crevices that are the width of a sheet of paper. They balance side by side, head to tail, upon the railings of the steps and spill out of sight.

I tell myself the mice are more afraid of me than I am of them, but then I spot what's really spooked them. From the unseen depths of the service area thirty feet below springs a blur of teeth and fur.

The deli cat alights.

Its mouth is pulled back, but I can't hear its hiss. The mice must have smelled it coming. The cat frolics in their fear. It flicks its copper-and-black-ringed tail. It balances on its hind legs. It paws at the air.

Falling forward onto all fours, it looks at me and runs its narrow pink tongue around the white fur that encircles its mouth. It raises a shoulder and then sets to stalking. It slinks back and forth along the length of the ledge, and as before, it never takes its eyes off of me. It dares me to raise the window and let it in.

This time, I do.

chapter five

The deli cat soars at me like a shot. It's a cannonball made of cotton. One second, it's on the landing; the next— KAPOOF!—it's on the bathroom windowsill. Without scraping its nails across cement, it has sailed through the damp night and dropped what must be twenty pounds without a thud. Up close, the cat is huge—not fat but tall and muscular. It doesn't have a belly that wags when it runs or balloons out when it sits on its haunches and studies you. Which is what it's doing to me now.

The window is opened half a foot. The cat's head is framed by one of eight small, square windowpanes. Its black mask gives it the appearance of an old-timey burglar. Its front feet line up between its back feet. Its considerable butt hovers behind it, but the weight doesn't throw the cat off balance. The cat looks like it could hold this position for the rest of its life.

An icy sideways breeze bends the cat's fur. I shiver. All I've got on is my Nada Surf hoodie and pajama shorts. The cat shifts. In that frigid moment of revelation, I see that *it* is a *he*.

I step back from the window and wave the cat in.

He ducks his head under the molding and dives toward the toilet. The lid is up. He adapts for a crash-landing and splays his four legs. His paws hit the porcelain doughnut. Straddling the water, the cat cranes his head up at me, perturbed.

He hops onto the edge of the tub. Saunters. The side of his body brushes the shower curtain. He turns his head every which way—up at Octavia's damp towel, at the medicine cabinet and sink past the end of the tub, at me. He cases the small joint.

I reach down to stroke his back.

The cat recoils. His head shrinks into his neck. His chin disappears into his chest fluff. But he doesn't hiss or take a swipe at me. I figure he's one of those cats who likes to be petted when *he* likes to be petted. One of Marjorie and Mags's Siamese cats is like that. Unlike Jelly, whom the twins' mom calls an *attention whore*, Peanut Butter wants nothing to do with you until he's snoring. (Yes, they do. Cats snore. When we spend the night at the twins', my sister shuts herself up in their shared bathroom to get away from the noise.) Pet Peanut Butter while he's awake, and you're going to get scratched. Before the twins accepted this, their fingers and forearms looked like they'd arm-wrestled a rosebush.

I mouth *Sorry* to the deli cat and raise my hands like it's a stickup.

He hops down, slinks toward the closed door, and scratches his cheeks across the bottom hinge. He purrs.

"Shh!" I whisper. "You are not getting into the rest of this apartment. Octavia will kill me if she sees you."

The cat purrs louder. He is a big cat and makes a suitably big noise.

I flap my hands. *Keep it down!*

The cat shuts up as if he understands English. Or sign language. Or my anxiety about waking my sister. Or giving my dad a reason to come in here. The cat's obedience is kind of cute. When does anyone ever do what I say?

He moves toward me. I'm pinned where I stand. I manage to take a step in reverse, but the toilet rim presses against the back of my bare knee. Frosty air gushes through the open window and finds its way down the neck of my sweatshirt.

The cat is a space heater. His nose is less than an inch from my shin. Maybe he's ready to be friends, but I no longer want to pet him. Every hair stands out from his every pore as if he is being electrocuted. He looks up at me and purrs like a cell phone on vibrate—no sound, but I hear it anyway. He rubs his cheek against my leg.

He is not soft. His hair is thick and coarse. My flesh tingles.

Now it's me who recoils.

The cat looks up at me again. His emerald eyes are real jewels glistening in the moonlight pouring through the open window. He blinks expectantly for my hand or my voice to encourage him.

"Good boy," I whisper.

He rubs his cheek against the same spot on my shin.

The tingling turns to an itch. I reach down to scratch. The

cat jerks his head out of the way of my hand. He wriggles backward and then sits to watch me watch him. My fingers hover above that patch of my skin, which feels as if it has been swabbed with honey, then plastered with fire ants. Maybe I'm allergic to cats. Aren't Peanut Butter and Jelly hypoallergenic? If my throat closes up and I have to go to the emergency room, I am going to be mortified because I haven't shaved my legs in a week. But when my fingernails make contact with the sore spot on my shin, I know I am hallucinating.

I don't feel stubble. I feel fur.

The cat's face is the same: friendly but expectant. He rises off his haunches and casually steps toward me.

I hiss. I want him out of here. I open my mouth and press the sides of my tongue against my top molars. I take a deep breath and then force that air out like one of our radiators. The cat is showered in my spittle.

He doesn't budge or blink those green eyes.

I hiss again.

The cat stays put.

I prop my foot on the tub and turn my shin to the moonlight.

There is a patch of fur beneath my kneecap the size and shape of a Post-it note. The fur isn't thick and coarse like the cat's. The texture is like chick's fuzz before it feathers, except, unlike the chick or the note, the fur on my leg isn't yellow. It's not copper, black, white, or any combination of the deli cat's calico mix. It is pumpkin orange.

I want the cat gone. I reach down to grab him.

He swats at me. Fast as fast, he rolls onto his back, and—one, two!—his front paws swipe the air between us. Unlike the chipped, Chanel Blue Satin–polished, squared nails of girls at Purser-Lilley, the deli cat's claws are pointed and flecked with dried blood.

Sorry! I stick 'em up again.

The deli cat flicks his tail. When it comes down, the long rope lashes the top of my left foot.

Tingling. The fire ants are back.

Across my foot, a diagonal line emerges. The strip of skin is pink, then red, then swollen. The strip blisters and pops but expels no liquid. The wound (rash?) is changing fast—too fast. Fine fuzzy orange fur sprouts out. I am frozen in fear.

The cat slides his front feet forward, lifts his rear end, and curls his tail toward his head. His haunches rise. He shuts his eyes because the stretch feels so good. His ecstasy lasts and lasts and lasts.

In his temporary blindness, I remember what the twins' mom does to their cats to clip their nails or get them into their carriers without a fight. I yank Octavia's damp towel off the shower rod and drop it over the deli cat like a tarp. He *mrowls!* Disoriented, he goes limp, and I scoop him up in the towel sack. With one hoist, I capture him in my arms. With one heave, I catapult him though the open bathroom window.

He drops from sight. I don't see him hit the back landing, but

I know he lands on his feet because I hear his claws grate the cement. I worry he'll spring back—attack! I grab the window and slam it shut.

It is this crash that wakes my sister. On the other side of the closed bathroom door, through the wool curtain encapsulating her bottom bunk bed, I hear Octavia's voice.

"Oh. No. You. Di'hint!"

I don't say a word. I slide down the wall, sit on the bath mat, and wait for her to fall back asleep.

But I fall asleep instead.

●　●　●

In the morning, I wake up with her towel balled beneath my cheek and her knuckles rapping against the bathroom door.

"I'll be out in a minute!"

Octavia says, "You've been in there all night! You know I need my sleep. I can't believe you woke me up."

"You woke yourself up! I came in here to get away from you. All night long, you were going on and on with your dream debate. *Harry Potter encourages the occult. Hogwarts promotes cohabitation and thus promiscuity. When Hermione gives herself a cat face, it means she has her period.*

"Oh, my God." My sister's voice lowers. "What else did I say?"

Other than *witch*, Octavia said nothing else. Fortunately, this one time, her debate topic is something I can fake my way through. I've never read Harry Potter, and Octavia knows this. But I've watched the movie trailers. And when it comes to book banning, I've seen my fair share. Burning books in Alabama is as popular as four-wheeling. When I lived there, you could forget about getting your hands on a copy of *Are You There God? It's Me, Margaret.* In the Bible belt, Judy Blume and J. K. Rowling are interchangeable. Their novels, along with any censored author's, contain one or more of the three M's: *m*agic, sexual *m*ischief, or *m*enstruation.

I hold my breath. There's no response. It's a pretty big moment: for the first time in our lives together, not only have I out-debated Octavia, but I have made her believe a complete and utter lie.

I turn on the shower and get in.

Now, this isn't one of those stories where I tell myself last night was all a bad dream—the whole thing with the mice and the cat and the fur, I mean. And I'm not going to stick my face in the shower spray, wash my hair, and go all Herbal Essence, then glance down at my legs, see that orange fluff, do a double take, and think, *Or was it?* The fur is there. I sense the patch like a headless pimple. There is a constant pressure of something foreign working its way out of my skin.

I grab my razor. I don't bother to lather up. I shave, swiping from ankle to knee. The Bic triple blades stick. I jerk the clogged razor away from my shin. The disposable head breaks off. It clatters and slides toward the drain. Instead of touching the fur myself, I examine it with the dull, curved, pink plastic handle.

The patch on my shin has not grown. The fine orange fuzz flattens under the water. Narrow strips of skin are visible between wet orange clumps. The stringy diagonal line on my left foot is also unchanged.

I decide then and there not to tell Octavia what's happened to me.

Why? Because Octavia will tell our parents. Hey, if the situation were reversed, I would too. It's what a good sister does when the other sister's in trouble. In the past, trouble meant passing out on a Pilates mat or getting harassed by a racist gym coach; trouble with Ling Ling or trouble understanding *The Yellow Wallpaper* in Fem Lit; troubles that could be dealt with or disregarded. Our parents are good at distinguishing which is which. But my current trouble is something they never bargained for when they adopted me. They were ready for acting out, for testing them, for the rebellion that will never happen. But this is worse than teen pregnancy. I let a strange, diseased cat into our house. I got myself sick. The fur is my fault. Hopefully, I can get rid of it before anyone notices. I'm not ready to show my parents the kind of freak I really am.

I mask the evidence with knee socks and put on the rest of my school uniform. When I come out of my bedroom, I find Octavia at the dining table, sitting before a tray full of small glasses of orange juice. Mom is sitting across from her with a notepad.

"Mary, look at you, all dressed and ready for school!" Mom believes if I look good, I am good. She's trying to forget my fever last night. Plus, she's convinced there's nothing a healthy breakfast won't cure. She asks, "Are you feeling well enough to help your sister pick the orange juice with the arsenic?"

Octavia gives me the same *can-you-believe-this?* look that the twins give us when their mother comes home with a face full of fresh Botox. I shrug. Everybody's parents are weird in their own ways.

Our mother is a cozy mystery writer. Cozies are for whodunit readers who like to cozy up with a good, not too graphically violent book about everyday heroines falling ass-backward into scenes of crimes. There's usually a pet involved, at least one love interest, and always a wacky best friend. Mom's amateur sleuth is Rebecca Starling, and her novels are set in 1930s Hollywood. Mom yearns for the return of girdles and white gloves. Marilyn Stasio, mystery-book critic for the *New York Times Book Review*, once wrote that Mom was better at describing what dead bodies wear than their causes of death. Since then, Mom has tested out methods to get away with murder.

She informs my sister and me that arsenic has an almond aftertaste and wants to know if we can taste the almond extract through the acidity of the OJ.

Octavia says to me, "Come on, belly up to the bar."

Happy to be distracted from my own troubles, I pick up a glass and take a sip.

chapter six

In gym class, Fridays are for noncompetitive cardio. *Just for fun,* Coach calls it. My idea of fun is staying put on the bleachers with Marjorie, Mags, and Octavia. Coach's idea of fun is anything she might have done at summer sports camp when the fields were rained out—emphasis on *anything.* Crab soccer, single-sex square dancing, you name it. Today is parachute day.

Nick Martin (yes, *the* Nick Martin) and Ben Strong have doctors' notes excusing them from further rope-climbing in the boys' gym, so they help our coach carry in an extra-large, folded parachute. The machismo of the boys' coach is legendary. Ling Ling Lebowitz has made a nice little business writing phony get-out-of-gym-free notes on her pediatrician mom's prescription pad. She sells or barters the notes to boys who aren't in peak physical shape or in the mood to hear their coach threaten to rip off their heads and take a dump down their necks.

Despite what his name might imply, Ben Strong is scrawny. His shorts reveal shredded inner thighs and calves from the many times his coach bullied him into climbing the rope. Nick's legs look okay to me—better than okay. So does the rest of him. What's he even doing here? Didn't he get what he needed from Ling Ling last night? I try not to stare.

Marjorie mutters, "Nick's eyes are bloodshot."

Octavia offers an explanation: "Recurring pinkeye."

"He doesn't have pinkeye," I say. "He was out late."

"How would you know?"

"Isn't everyone out late besides us?"

I'm not going to tell the girls about spying on Nick and Ling Ling by the bus stop. If I tell them, they'll ask me what the two of them were doing. I'll have to describe Ling Ling wrapped in Nick's arms. I'll have to admit there's something so alluring about her that Nick was willing to share her with three other boys. I'll ramble on about the connection I felt to him when he couldn't possibly have known he was looking at me. I'll tell them about the deli cat. About my shin and my foot. I'll spill my guts out for everyone to see. Thanks but no thanks. I'll keep myself to myself.

The boys lay the parachute across most of the gym floor, stretching it out in a humongous circle. Judging from their huffing and puffing, it's heavy—the type of chute used to drop a year's worth of supplies to missionaries in the middle of nowhere. Mustard yellow, it's painted with the world's largest Have-a-Nice-Day face.

I take a position in front of a big, black dot eye. Marjorie and Mags stand to my right. Octavia stands to my left. Ling Ling is across from us, centered in front of the no-lipped smile. Other girls fill in the arcs in between. When Coach blows her whistle, we bend over and grab hold of the thick seam.

Coach cries, "Shake it, ladies!"

Gripping the seam at our hips, we move our arms up and down, up and down, fast, like we're fanning flames. The parachute flaps, the happy face warps, and the beating material fills the gym with claps of thunder. It is such ludicrous exercise that we crack up. We feel ten years old, except everyone's boobs are shaking, and those of us who don't have boobs stand out even more.

Ling Ling's hard, round B-cups are so vacuous, the cups dent. Flapping, she has no real breasts to stop the underwire from riding up. Her faux breasts are at her neck. She has no idea what's happened, and smiles at the boys. Ben gawks. Nick avoids the spectacle that is Ling Ling by focusing on the faded squares on the wall where team photos and plaques used to hang before sports were banned. Even though most of us girls don't like Ling Ling, we are mortified for her. That is, all of us except for Octavia, who looks like she thinks Ling Ling's getting the fate she deserves. My sister's just as flat-chested as Ling Ling and me but opts for camisoles instead of not-so-wonderful bras to avoid such a scenario. How long have we been shaking this thing?

"My arms are killing me!" I shout.

"Your arms?" shouts Coach, who's walking massive circles around us and has timed it perfectly to hear me complain. "In those dress socks, you should worry about the pain your nose is going to be in, Mary Richards!"

To avoid exposing my fuzzy shin and foot when changing for gym class, I'd said I left my gym socks at home. To avoid using a pair of extras the coach keeps in a wicker basket on the corner of her desk, I swore I'd rather die. The coach has no patience for hysterics. As long as I participated in today's activities, she claimed that she didn't care if I worked out in my plaid skirt and cardigan. I didn't go that far. I'm flapping my arms like crazy in white shorts and a Purser-Lilley T-shirt. I'm in sneakers. Only my socks aren't athletic. Sweat has soaked through the wool.

Coach says, "Put some muscle into it, ladies! Up and over!"

We lift the parachute over our heads and then twist and drop to our knees, bringing the rim of the parachute to the floor so we are encapsulated in a stuffy, echoing igloo. We beat the seam against the unused (but twice-monthly waxed) basketball court. Above us, the parachute wavers like a jaundiced jellyfish.

"All together, ladies!" The coach blows her whistle. *Tweet-tweet, tweet-tweet!* "Keep tempo with your neighbor!"

Nick's shadow is cast against the parachute. He's right in front of me. I know it's him. Ben's shadow would be skinnier. The coach's would have an outline of a discontinued Purser-Lilley softball cap and a clipboard. If I took one hand off the seam and pressed my fingers against the parachute, I could touch Nick. Before I work up the courage, I'm struck in the head.

I topple backward. The parachute seam gaps in my empty spot. Laid out, I glimpse Nick's sneakers: red Chuck Taylor high tops, laces undone.

Octavia turns around to help me up, and her head and shoulders graze the underside of the parachute.

Coach shouts: "Ladies, back in place! Pump those arms! Keep the parachute up! Gentlemen, do not throw the tennis balls directly at the ladies! This isn't dodge ball! Your directive is to make the parachute collapse! Throw the tennis balls at the top, along the sides, above the ladies' heads! We may not be allowed to play tennis at this school, but by God, we will use the sports equipment your parents' good money once paid for! These are perfectly good tennis balls! Put 'em in the air!"

Tweet-tweet!

A hailstorm of tennis balls pummels the parachute. Nick's shadow hurls the balls and then chases after them when they bounce off. Ben's shadow whips by, throwing double-handed while he's in motion. He collects two balls with each hand every time he bends over. When he throws them, they split in four different directions, but all four balls strike the parachute. Ben moves so fast that if his pipe cleaner–thin thighs weren't so far apart, they'd chafe.

Octavia marvels, "Who knew he had it in him?" She stretches her arms wide to cover my place.

I scoot to the center. Don't ask me why. It's a rare opportunity and a cool thing to do. The world's largest Have-a-Nice-Day face warbles high above me as the rest of the girls struggle to keep it inflated. Elbows pump like pistons. Knuckles bang against the floor. I'm inside a stove-top Jiffy Pop popper, but the popcorn's on the outside. Tennis balls keep coming. Girls have sunk from their knees onto their butts. Ponytails stick to damp T-shirts. Everyone's back is to me. No one besides my sister knows where I am until the coach shouts, "Cease fire! Cease fire! Ladies, up and over!"

Girls scramble to their feet, swing the parachute above their heads, and toss it backward so it will plunge to land at their heels. As the parachute descends upon me, I spy Nick spy me. My panic registers on his face. Before everything goes black (or mustard yellow, to be exact), he falls forward into a push-up position and rolls toward me, under the seam, before the parachute hits the floor.

We're covered. Trapped. Nick clutches my wrist.

I turn my head but don't see him. The deflated parachute has filled in the space between us. There is not a lot of air. I won't waste my breath. I wriggle my wrist to signal him that I'm okay.

The coach blows her whistle: three short tweets, then three long, then three short. Maybe she thinks all Purser-Lilley kids spend weekends watching Turner Classic Movies and learned Morse code for SOS from Inspector Poirot in *Death on the Nile*. It doesn't take the coach long to figure out that in case of emergency, her students only know how to respond by whipping out their cell phones. If I suffocate, I bet Ling Ling will use my death to spearhead a movement to get cell phones reinstated.

Coach shouts, "Help them!"

You'd think the girls would return to their spots along the seam and lift the parachute off of us like a manhole cover. Nope. Some decide to take hold and drag it off. Others get the same brilliant idea but take hold of the other side. They have themselves a tug-of-war. Pulled taut, the parachute is close to the floor. It slides back and forth. Girls' feet slip under the surface. The material is abrasive. My hair, full of static, clings to it. Nick and I rock and roll from the friction beneath the parachute until I am rolled completely on top of him.

My back aligns with his chest. His muscular thighs rub the backs of mine. His breath raises me up. I am bound, but I'm floating. Oh, my God, to be this close to Nick Martin! This isn't the way I imagined it would be, but I'll take it. I pray we never get out from under this. Sure, it will be a strange compromised life, but I can live with it.

Nick spits out a chunk of my hair.

Coach shouts, "Boy!"

Obviously, since Purser-Lilley doesn't let us have coed gym, there is no way our double lump under the parachute is allowed.

Nick fidgets.

My socks start to inch their way down. My orange fur itches to get out. If Nick sees what I'm hiding, I'll never stand a chance with him. If Ling Ling sees, I'll never hear the end of it. I can't let my socks come off.

I throw my body into Pilates teaser pose, which is me sending legs and arms up, as straight as rigor mortis, so I look like a V. All my weight sinks into Nick's gut. He squirms. I flail and claw to escape my yellow hell. I flip to my hands and knees, belly-crawl to the light. Gasping for breath, I rise to meet the rest of the girls' slack-jawed stares. From the outside of the parachute, Nick and I must have looked like two Mexican jumping beans in a pea pod. Kinky.

"Yum, yum, gimme some!" a voice howls in delight.

You can guess whose sister said that. I don't even bother looking toward Octavia, who is doubled over laughing and pretending to try to get a grip on herself.

The twins' porcelain-doll complexions burn the palest of pinks.

Ben and the coach grapple to peel the crumpled parachute off Nick. His eyes are squeezed shut. I've knocked the wind out of him. Does he feel the weight of the girls' collective scrutiny upon him like another parachute? His breath slows. His chest rattles. His face slackens. He snorts. Or is that a snore?

"Asleep like Mary was yesterday!" cries Ling Ling. "Mary's so contagious, she's a walking canker sore!"

"Watch your mouth, Lebowitz," Coach says. "This is your one warning."

Ben kicks the toe bumper of Nick's untied sneaker. That jars him. He springs to his feet.

"Sorry, Coach," he says calmly—as if he wasn't laid out under me under a deflated parachute nor snuck in a ten-second nap afterward.

Coach says, "There is a time and a place for heroics, but this is neither here nor then. I know you were trying to help, but the best intentions can get you in hot water."

"Hot water?" cries Ling Ling. "If anyone should be sterilized, it's Mary! Now Nick's got whatever she's giving!"

Tweet! "Lebowitz!" Coach barks. "Take a lap!"

Disgruntled, Ling Ling sprints around the perimeter of the gym. Her short bob, bleached blond last weekend without her mother's permission, wags at her chin. Her blunt bangs bounce. At home, before the start of every school day, she applies a lipstick shade that is banned at Purser-Lilley. She gets away with it because she doesn't bring the tube onto school property. The color doesn't need to be reapplied. For twelve hours, her lips are stained Cranberry C***. When she comes full circle, her frown is more pronounced than any foul thing she might say.

Ling Ling overdramatically swabs her dry brow with an arm of her long-sleeve T. She bends over, braces her hands on her knees, and gives the boys an eyeful of her short shorts.

"Keep running!" shouts Coach. To Ben, she says, "You are excused."

Ben asks, "But what about your big thing and balls?"

He's talking about the sports equipment, but the twins'

pink faces turn mauve. Their scalps radiate under their colorless hair. Octavia opens her mouth to crack wise about something—the comment, the twins, Ben, our bleach-blond arch-nemesis—but reconsiders at the sight of Ling Ling in motion. Coach let Octavia get away with *Yum, yum, gimme some.* Unlike Ling Ling, however, my sister knows when to not push her boundaries.

Coach glances at the parachute heap. She surveys the gym floor, littered with hundreds of tennis balls. Some quiver beneath the overhead heating ducts. If the tennis balls were land mines, none of us would make it out of here alive.

She says to Ben, "You've helped enough. You're released. Go back to the boys' gym and dress out."

"Yes, Coach." Ben shuffles toward the exit. He collides with Ling Ling, who gestures to his rope-burned legs and says something that we can't hear but must be brutal. He hangs his head and skulks out.

Coach shouts, "Ling Ling Lebowitz, if you can talk, you are not running fast enough! Nick, I want a word. The rest of you, start picking up balls!"

I ask, "What about me?"

Octavia gives me a look that says, *Girl, you be buggin'.*

Coach gives me a look that says, *You are an accident that's already happened.* She doesn't mean this the way Ling Ling would if she'd said it. Coach is having mercy on me. I've embarrassed myself enough: the socks, the parachute, the outburst, the boy.

I should do myself a favor, put my head down, pick up balls, and blend in.

Coach says to Nick, "Don't be such a hero next time. If you're injured, it's my responsibility. From what I know, coaches around here get fired for hurting feelings."

Nick catches sight of me. He looks through the coach like he looked through my parents' blinds. His eyes don't change like Octavia's did when her expression told me I was bugging or like the coach's did when she let me know I'd embarrassed myself enough. Nick's eyes are steady, perfect ovals. I get lost in their darkness.

Sneakers stop scuffling across the court. Ling Ling pauses in my peripheral vision. Everyone's staring at Nick and me because we are staring at each other. For how long? Five seconds? Five minutes? I don't know. I don't care. Nick is trying to tell me something. I feel it physically, as if his hand is still clutching my wrist. I keep my sights on him until I read him loud and clear: if I am ever in danger, he will defy Coach's orders, ignore Ling Ling's barbs, and get by anyone in his way to save me.

Ling Ling races toward us but is stalled by the coach. "What?" Ling Ling challenges her, panting for real. She stops a foot away from me, but her legs keep on pumping. "I'm doing my laps, Coach! I'm lapping in place!"

Coach's eyes flash from her to Nick and then rest on me. She asks, "Ling Ling Lebowitz, what business is this of yours?"

"My boyfriend's my business!"

Nick doesn't deny it.

Coach says, "I don't care if you two are Mr. and Mrs. *Dr. Phil.* This is my gym!"

I don't hear what either Coach or Ling Ling says after that. Or what Nick doesn't say. The dress-out bell rings. I head toward the locker room. At the door, other girls crowd behind me. They want me to move faster, so I do. But it's really something else that compels me forward. That something is so enticing, I forget about Nick and what we just shared.

chapter seven

There is a smell you wouldn't expect coming from the locker room. I'm not going to describe the additional smells you would expect. If you're not home-schooled, you can list the smells for yourself.

Girls rush past me as I stand motionless, sniffing, trying to identify what the special smell is. We have fifteen minutes to change before our next class. Marjorie grabs a clean towel from the cubbies and tosses it to me. I toss the towel to Mags because I am not stripping off these knee socks to jump in the communal shower.

Octavia has a free period after gym. She sits on a bench to wait for the rest of our class to clear out so she can shower in private. No one at Purser-Lilley, including me, has ever seen her bare torso. Freshman year, Ling Ling got detention for saying that my sister had *Thug Life* tattooed across her stomach. Octavia didn't dignify the accusation with a response or raise her camisole to prove it wrong, but I could tell she was hurt. So, she's super self-conscious about her body—so what? That's not the worst thing in the world. I join her in front of our lockers.

I ask, "Don't you smell that?"

"Smell what? Your pheromones? What was up with you and Nick?"

I ignore her. I don't want to talk about him. Even if I did, I couldn't. The smell in here is too distracting. "It smells herbal, like one of Mom's poisons."

Octavia stares at me with either impatience or worry. "I don't smell anything."

I wave my cupped hand under my nose.

Octavia pinches hers. She says, "Eau de B.O."

"We're sitting on top of it."

"It's your socks."

"It's not my socks." I cross my ankle over my knee, bend forward, and take a whiff to make sure. My sweaty socks don't smell good, but they're not what I'm after. I sit up. "It's coming from one of the lockers."

Steam filters through our small alleyway of narrow metal doors. Soon, the alley will be jam-packed with girls in their underwear. Deodorant, lotion, and perfume will be applied and overpower the mystery scent I am compelled to root out. I lean forward and press my nose to the nearest locker grate.

"That's my locker, Nancy Drew."

I scoot over and press my nose to another locker. I smell cigarettes. Which one of my classmates sneaks smokes on the side? I scoot again and smell Listerine. Who has gingivitis? I hear one of the squeaky shower knobs turn off. I scoot farther and smell "deodorized" tampons and pads. Girls' voices grow clearer as less and less water runs to drown them out. I scoot yet again and smell more sanitary stuff. The other girls will be back any second. I'm running out of options. As I press my nose to the grate of the last locker, I nearly tumble off the end of the bench.

I've found it.

Whatever the odor is, it is rich, earthy, and intoxicating. I want to spread it out on the floor like an emptied suitcase full of money and roll around in it so I can bask in it all day long. Purser-Lilley uses the honor code, which means no locks on our lockers. When I pull up the handle and stick my hands inside to grope for the source, Octavia gasps. So does everyone else who has come back in time to see me try to steal from Ling Ling.

Don't worry—she's not standing right behind me. Forty-some witnesses are dramatic enough. Ling Ling's still on the defunct basketball court with the coach and what's-his-name.

Octavia is on her feet and has her hand on my elbow. The rest of the girls huddle together as if they're watching a horror show. I guess what I'm doing is pretty horrific. Except for the elbow my sister holds, I've fit every part of my body inside Ling Ling's locker.

With a jerk, I wriggle out of Octavia's grasp. The locker is confining but tall. I turn in circles, knocking Ling Ling's clothes off hooks. Between my feet is her gigantic purse, printed with the current must-have designer's initials. The bag is blood-red dyed lambskin and retails for five grand. Ling Ling didn't get her sweet sixteen birthday party, but she got her non-returnable, wait list–worthy present. If she'd asked for a puppy, she could fit a litter inside.

I draw my hands into the namaste yoga salutation, then dive, twisting myself into a folded position: fingers at my toes, forehead to my knees. Thanks to Pilates, I am as limber as a contortionist in Cirque du Soleil.

I unzip Ling Ling's bag.

The smell explodes! It smells *so* good. As long as I keep inhaling it, I don't care what happens to me. I rifle and find a cosmetic bag, a pencil bag, a battered paperback, hair clips, straw wrappers, plastic spoons, and wadded receipts from Pinkberry, Jamba Juice, and Tasti D-Lite. I pull out the cosmetic bag, unzip it, and sniff. I do the same with the pencil bag. There's nothing in either that you wouldn't expect. I flick both small bags out of the locker, forgetting that my sister is blocking the door.

Octavia says: "Have you lost your damn mind?" But she is finished trying to stop me. She's as curious as I am to see what I dig out. I locate a zipper along the inside of the purse. I jerk it and hear the tiny brass teeth separate. The teeth scratch my knuckles when I shove my hand into the pouch. There's one object in there. I wrap my hand around it and yank it free.

Until this point, no one has called for the coach because: a) they want to see crazy go crazier; or b) they want to see

Ling Ling go crazy when she finds out what I've done. No one likes Ling Ling enough to stop me from going through her things. No one calls for the coach yet because they want to see what Ling Ling is hiding. If Coach comes, she'll confiscate whatever it is. On the other hand, if the coach comes, she'll bring Ling Ling in tow. Ling Ling will have a legitimate reason to chew me out and rip me a new one. She will kick one hundred percent of my ass. *Fight! Fight!* Every girl wants to scream it once in her life. To guarantee they get their chance, the girls finally shout for the coach.

Coach appears in an instant. She's not allowed to teach wrestling, but she hasn't forgotten her Vulcan nerve pinch. She clamps her thumb and all four opposing fingers to the nape of my neck. I go limp. She ducks me out of the locker, grabs the pulse point at the end of my forearm, and applies pressure. It doesn't hurt, but my fingers bloom.

Ling Ling makes a grab for the small, gold, round tin that sits in the palm of my hand. The coach gets to it first. Whatever I've found must be worse than red lipstick with a dirty name.

The coach says, "Mary Richards, what do you have to say for yourself?"

I shriek, "Smell it! Don't you smell it?"

The coach brings the tin to her nose. "Strawberries."

"It's not strawberries," I say.

Ling Ling says, "It is! It's lip balm. Everybody has it!"

I recognize the red vine printed across the lid. It's the same brand my sister uses. The twins use it too. I don't because the smell is too artificial. It doesn't smell like strawberries. That pink stuff smells pink. But whatever is in Ling Ling's tin doesn't smell like fruit or color to me. How can the coach be fooled? She shakes her head at me but twists open the lid. Judging by how wide her eyes get, I was right about what's not inside. Even if you don't smoke it, you should be able to identify that small, dull, brownish-green clump.

"Ling Ling Lebowitz, marijuana is grounds for expulsion."

Girls clutch their towels above their chests and push forward to see.

Coach blows her whistle, but Ling Ling screams over the shrillness, "It's not mine! I'm holding it for Nick!"

This shuts everyone up.

Footsteps fill the silence, running fast away from the locker-room door, toward the main gym exit across the basketball court. Rubber soles—Nick's. He is repeatedly tripped by shoelaces, untied.

Dang it if I don't run after him.

Behind me, I hear Octavia: "What the—?"

I never hear the curse she inserts. I've squeezed through Coach and Ling Ling, shoved through the girls, sprung out of the locker room, and I am now close to halfway across the gym. I'm hurdling with nothing to hurdle. I feel like I could leap from the foul line all the way to the exit. Energy surges through me. My legs won't be stopped.

Coach shouts, "Slow down!"

I slip on the floor wax and slide into a pyramid of yoga blocks. Showered with dull foam edges, I don't feel any pain.

"Mary Richards, what has gotten into you?"

Am I high? Is this what high feels like? Can you get high without smoking? I thought pot was supposed to relax you. I am not relaxed! I get up. I have to catch Nick and make him answer my questions. Why did he look at me that way? Why is he dating Ling Ling? Was she really holding his weed for him? Since when does Nick smoke? Since when does Ling Ling? What's so special about her? What's so special about me? Barreling forward, I am fueled by curiosity.

When I reach Nick, he's at the principal's office door, confessing.

"Ling Ling made me trade it for one of her mom's fake doctor's notes."

"Her *what*? For *what*?" The principal frets. His chin—or rather, chins—blotch. Principal Sheldon is a thin man, but his neck is that of a man who was once fat.

Coach arrives with Ling Ling and explains the situation. I'm on the outer rim of the conversation—there but not there. Still, Principal Sheldon seems to understand that I broke into Ling Ling's locker and that this offense is on par with the hidden marijuana. The coach escorts herself back to the gym, leaving Principal Sheldon to call our in-case-of-emergency numbers. Turns out Dr. Lebowitz is in surgery. Mom's inaccessible in her writing studio, and Dad can't get away from the news desk. My parents will be here at the end of the day for Octavia's debate, so it's decided that the principal will talk with them then. In the meantime, in lieu of Nick's parents, who are out of the country on their annual winter getaway, his Greek grandparents totter in.

Nick's *yiayia* is draped in an oversized mink that smells like mothballs. Her hands are tucked inside an ancient muff. She removes nothing as she takes the seat her husband pulls out for her. Nick's *papou* opts to stand along with the rest of us. The principal shoos Ling Ling and me out of his office, but Yiayia objects.

She says, "These girls are why our Nick is in such trouble. They should stay and see what fate befalls him."

The principal says, "Mrs. Martin, the girls will be counseled separately."

"Mrs. *Martin* is my daughter-in-law. When she married my son, she changed his name and my grandson's name for her reasons. Me, *I* am Mrs. *Poulikakos*."

"Mrs...." Principal Sheldon won't risk mispronunciation, so he doesn't say it. He explains, "It is school procedure that offenders are met with individually. I will meet with the parents of Miss Lebowitz and Miss Richards—"

"Oh, these names you can say, but mine is such a hardship!"

Insulted, she extends her hand for her husband to hoist her out of her seat. I swear, her fur coat bristles. My leg and foot suddenly itch. I lean forward to scratch, but my head spins like

I'm having a combination sugar and caffeine crash. I sit back on the windowsill. My gym shorts ride up. Yiayia cuts her eyes at me. I've never been looked at with such disdain. Her mink has her stuck in the chair. Papou scoops her under the armpits. He pulls. She shrieks as if every brittle bone will dislocate and break.

"Fine, fine!" the principal says. "Everyone stay where they are. Nick, out with it."

Nick says, "I have asthma."

Ling Ling glares at him. Does she hate to hear the flaw uttered out loud? I am surprised I never knew about it. Nick's never had an asthma attack at school. The condition makes him a little less normal. He's not too skinny, not too fat, not too tall, not too short. He's got nice legs and deep, dark eyes. But, lo and behold, there's something about himself that he keeps to himself. What other secrets of Nick's does Ling Ling share? For one, that she's his girlfriend. And why was that a secret? Ling Ling's mean, but since when has meanness been a dating deterrent?

Papou explains, "The asthma affects our Nick only at night. But it keeps him from sleeping. You want him to do cartwheels, rotate the handstands, in a condition like his? *Nico mou* is exhausted. He didn't want to confess to his true life affliction or be bullied by your drill sergeant of a coach, so he white-lied—said he had a cold or cholera or whatever the girl wrote on her mother's pad. He took care of himself the best way he knew how. He was right to take the excuse from the girl."

The girl. Ling Ling shifts her glare to Papou. Well, what did she expect him to call her, his future granddaughter-in-law? Or is her relationship with Nick a secret from his family too?

The principal says, "Excuse or no excuse, your grandson brought an illegal substance onto school grounds. Nick, where did you get it?"

"From us," says Papou.

Principal Sheldon's chins quiver. "From you?"

Papou nods. "Please—his mother does not know. We keep it in the spice rack, in the oregano jar."

Yiayia states flatly: "His mother does not cook."

Turns out Nick's grandparents are potheads who take pride in growing their own in the lowlands of Mount Parnitha. Every Christmas, they come to New York for two months and smuggle a big plastic bag of it through customs. They use airport security profiling to their advantage. Papou plays the part of the kindly, loving, but exasperated husband while his wife shrieks in Greek as customs inspectors plow through her meticulously ironed and folded clothes. Customs inspectors never have the patience or stamina to make it through what the Poulikakoses bring with them. September 11 changed nothing for them in regards to how they travel. Instead of suitcases, they pack ten to twelve mini-boxes from the local agora. The boxes are taped and tied together with butcher's string and bungee cords. Finding the pot is like finding the million dollars on *Deal or No Deal*: an all-but-guaranteed impossibility.

"But what about drug-sniffing police dogs?" Principal Sheldon asks, mostly out of bafflement. His anger has faded.

Yiayia laughs at him. She clutches the handle of her purse like a roller-coaster safety bar as she rocks onto the back legs of her chair.

Papou says, "Dogs are for Colombians, Jamaicans. JFK is not so concerned with our little oregano."

Principal Sheldon says, "We are not talking about a little oregano. We are talking about breaking the law. Risking arrest. The rest of your lives in prison. Not to mention setting a bad example for Nick."

"For us, to help our only grandson is a privilege." Papou chokes up, waves off a box of tissues. "It is right. We have no choice. To see him suffer is not for us. What we bring to him is natural. From the earth."

"Like a cucumber!" exclaims Yiayia.

"*Nai,* like a cucumber," says Papou. "A cucumber takes the bags from under your eyes. It hydrates you when you have no water to drink. Sir, what we bring Nick helps him to sleep. *Medicinal* is how I think that you call it."

"How can you encourage a young man with asthma to smoke?"

"No smoke," says Yiayia. "Brownies! I hide the good stuff like pureed spinach!"

Nick's neck reddens. He's embarrassed, either because his yiayia has to trick him into eating his vegetables or because he can't take a toke like a man—I'm not sure which. Ling Ling seems turned off by the whole half-baked scenario. But this makes me more curious about who Nick really is. After the way he stopped, dropped, and rolled for me under the parachute, he's obviously no burnout. No wheezing invalid either. Hidden pot, closeted asthma, girlfriend on the sly—none of this makes sense.

I look to Nick, and there are those eyes: steady, perfect ovals. Again, I'm lost in their darkness. I have no sense of how much time is passing. A clock ticks on the wall. A bell rings for next period. Then, his invisible hand grips my wrist. Before he blinks and breaks our bond, I get the message: I am surrounded by lies.

The principal says, "Your grandson must have an inhaler."

Yiayia mutters, "This is no good."

"Mr. and Mrs..."

"*Poulikakos!*"

"*Madam.*" Principal Sheldon looks her in the eyes. "What you do in the privacy of your own home is not my concern. Western...Grecian...ancient medicine—that's up to you. But when a student brings marijuana into my school and shares it with my students, we have a problem."

Papou says, "You will never again have this problem from Nick."

"Sir, I want to believe you."

"Believe him," says Yiayia. "It is best that you do. You expose Nico mou, your Purser-Lilley parents will do away with right to privacy as they did with team sports. There will be security guards, random searches to conduct, the testing of urine.

Consider your future, sir. The rest of your school life riddled with interruptions. All because of a little oregano."

● ● ●

Nick got let off with a warning and a week's detention.

Ling Ling got two.

Dr. Lebowitz protested until she learned that her daughter had gotten time for both drug possession and masterminding a P.E. black market. Like any good mastermind, Ling Ling didn't name names, and the principal didn't press her. If he had, half the boys at Purser-Lilley would get detention. When Ling Ling's hall locker was raided, Principal Sheldon confiscated Dr. Lebowitz's prescription pad, last year's sophomore trig and biology final exams, three bags of Haribo gummy twin cherries, and an IOU from Ben Strong for a C-note.

Me, I got a lecture. Before I opened my mouth to defend myself, the principal copped a plea for me. If it hadn't been for my killer curiosity, he would never have known about what was going on right under his nose.

chapter eight

Kathryn Ann holds court at the head of three tables-for-two shoved together at Pizzeria Uno. She, the twins, my parents, my sister, and I are finishing our unlimited soup for supper and reliving how the Purser-Lilley debate team destroyed the Nightingale girls. My visit to the principal's office wears heavy on my parents' faces, but they are giving Octavia her moment of glory. During the debate, she brought one of her opponents to tears. Ben Strong, normally a fact-gatherer not a verbal assailant, reduced another girl to running off the stage as her rebuttal. Instant disqualification! My sister was impressed—but not as impressed as Kathryn Ann is with me.

She drawls, "Mary, hon, you are a star. If more people got involved with bustin' drugs, this country would be a safer place."

If you've watched *Chime In with Kathryn Ann*, you know she blames drugs for all of society's ills. According to her, if people didn't do drugs, they wouldn't be poor. There wouldn't be birth defects. The murder rate, which to her includes vehicular manslaughter, would plummet. Drugs lead to stealing, and stealing leads to bullets and knives. Drugs are depressants, and depressed people rape. Kathryn Ann is a teetotaler. I've never seen her so much as dip a fork into a pot of white wine-laden cheese fondue.

She says, "Who's Mama's little narc? Mary is! Yay, Mary!"

Octavia looks embarrassed for the twins. I don't blame her.

Mom says, "I'm worried about our Mary."

"Oh, my word," Kathryn Ann chuckles. "What is there to worry about? Your Mary's not on drugs."

"She's not herself lately."

"Mom, I'm fine," I say, but I am in fact worried sick.

Kathryn Ann says, "All Miss Mary needs is a night in with her friends. The girls are scheduled to spend the night at our place tonight. Let 'em. Their highfalutin school is a pressure cooker. No wonder your Mary snapped."

"She ran a fever last night," Dad says. "I think she should come home with us."

"Dad, I'm fine." I'm not fine, of course, but I don't want to go home. If I go home, I'll be watched. At the twins' apartment, I'll be free of parental supervision. Their dad's away on business three weeks of every month. *Chime In* airs live in two hours, so Kathryn Ann will be gone. I'm not sure what I'm planning on doing, but I won't get away with anything if I go home with my folks. They love me too much to leave me alone.

Kathryn Ann signals for the check. "Don't even think about splitting the bill, Scott. This is my treat. We're celebrating your two girls' major accomplishments. Besides, we're getting off easy. Free refills! Do you know how much my three Diet Cokes would cost anywhere else?"

"Twelve dollars," recite the twins. They know this like they know how much Triscuits cost without a coupon ($5.00) or how much a practically free box of name brand cereal costs without 1,500 D'Agastino green points ($6.00). Their mom likes to remind them she wasn't born with a silver spoon in her mouth, and now that she's got one, she's not about to spit it out. Life is unpredictable. Money isn't. If Kathryn Ann and her husband drop dead, the twins need to manage what took her a lifetime to secure.

Kathryn Ann hefts her blood-red designer bag onto her shoulder. It's the same Upper East Side must-have as Ling Ling's, but Kathryn Ann got hers gratis from the designer's publicity department. They wanted her to be photographed with it, but I doubt they wanted it to be while she was coming out of Pizzeria Uno. She tells my parents, "Quit your worrying. I'll drop the girls off at our place and send Mary back to you tomorrow better than new. Trust me, she and Octavia will be perfectly fine. Have a date night!"

Dad nudges Mom. "There's a double feature at the Film Forum." Mom begrudgingly agrees.

Upon reaching the twins' Fifth Avenue apartment building a few blocks away, a town car is waiting to take their mom to the TV studio. Kathryn Ann clips coupons and never eats anywhere with a coat check but doesn't take public transportation? She sees how puzzled I am. Ducking into the back seat, she says, "This ain't my money, honey." She winks and points to her tight face. "And neither is this!"

It's the cable channel's directive that Kathryn Ann continue to be "fresh" at fifty-eight years old. She told them that if that's what they wanted, then they'd have to pay for it.

We wave good-bye, and a doorman walks us to the front entrance. Another doorman opens one of the double doors from inside. Another doorman meets us in the entryway and walks us to the elevator. Another doorman holds the elevator door open for us as we fit ourselves inside with him. Yes, that's right: four doormen for the four of us. The final doorman presses the PH button and takes us to the top.

The elevator opens into a tiny receiving area hardly bigger than the elevator itself. There is a sideboard for mail and, to the left, enough room for an umbrella stand filled with bright red promotional umbrellas that, when you open them, have tiny bells dangling from the spokes that read *Chime In!*

Despite the building's staff of twenty-three, the apartment is locked. The twins have a key but also a pass code that must be punched in within fifteen seconds of unlocking the door to silence an alarm. Mags fishes in her book bag for her key chain, while Marjorie readies her fingers over the pad.

But then they simultaneously freeze.

"What?" Octavia whispers.

The twins are more attuned to their surroundings than we

are and thus must have picked up on what my sister and I are now hearing. From the depths of their apartment, the noise is getting closer.

Crying.

Terrible, terrible, terrible crying.

When the twins open the door, Peanut Butter and Jelly are standing on the threshold and screaming. It's not meowing. I've heard these two cats "talk" before and even "yell" at each other when they play-fight, but what they sound like now are inconsolable babies. Their slick, cream-colored hair stands on end. Their backs arch. The centers of their spines are level with their pointy black ears. Their tails puff. Their trimmed claws are out, curled downward. The blunt tips dig into the hardwood like thirty-six tiny sickles. Their black paws hover above the floor.

"Peanut Butter!" admonishes Mags.

"Jelly!" Marjorie says.

Octavia shrinks into the far corner of the receiving area. She hugs her book bag to her chest. She shuts her eyes and prays—as if God will stop what he's doing, reach down, pinch her collar, and airlift her back to 72nd and Lex.

My sister has a fear of cats. She usually keeps it in check around Peanut Butter and Jelly but refuses to be left alone with them. Up until now, they've never done anything I'd consider scary. Peanut Butter only swats at you if you get up in his grill. I always figured Octavia was irrationally scared of cats like other people are scared of snakes and spiders. That's the thing about living with someone you haven't known your whole life. You never truly know what's going to freak that person out, how badly, or when.

Octavia slams the heel of her hand against the elevator button. She beats it. If I didn't know any better, I would think she's going to break it or jam the elevator car. The twins and I gape at her, momentarily forgetting the braying cats. The elevator arrow ticks, pausing sporadically between numbers 1 and 14 as it crawls toward PH. The crying and pounding must be echoing down the shaft.

The call button light goes out. I hear the car rising into place. In five seconds, the door will open, and the twins' mom will never forgive them for exposing the secret that they're harboring cats. This building doesn't allow pets. Kathryn Ann tips the doormen extra every Christmas to look the other way. If anyone from a lower floor has come along to investigate what's going on up here, the twins are in big trouble. Marjorie and Mags grab hold of Octavia and drag her into their apartment.

The cats scatter. I scoot in after them and pull the door shut.

We hear the elevator door slide open and a doorman give a nosy neighbor the brush-off. "Babies? No ma'am. I didn't hear any babies."

The elevator door closes, and away they go.

The cats come back. They slink silently, shoulder to shoulder, a pack of two. The fur on one side of each of their pale necks is wet. Kathryn Ann's house policy is to leave the kitchen sink barely running so that her "darlings" can tilt their heads under the skinny stream and drink fresh water whenever they want. I wonder what it's like for the twins to live with Peanut Butter and Jelly, another set of siblings who are older than they are but never grew up.

The cats slither toward me.

"Boys!" says Marjorie. "What is wrong with you?"

They sniff my knee socks, sniff my shoes. Do they smell the orange fuzz? Of course they do. I stiffen like a stop sign. To me, the fuzz smells like the rest of me. To Peanut Butter and Jelly, it must smell unnatural. They must be trying to figure out if I'm friend or foe. Or too sick to stay near.

Marjorie says, "Boys, you know Mary. It's Mary!"

Mags says, "She must have gotten that pot on her socks."

"Since when do cats like pot?" asks Marjorie.

"Since it's all-natural. You know how they like to eat grass."

Octavia tries to show signs of her old self. "Yo, your cats love the chronic," she jokes weakly, but her skin is devoid of brightness.

Peanut Butter and Jelly rub their wet necks against my socks.

"See?" says Marjorie. "It's Mary!"

Kitchen sink water from the cats' necks soaks through the wool. The cats purr. Their vibrations tickle. The brothers are slender, but when they lean against the outsides of my lower legs, their combined pressure makes me feel like I'm going to collapse. Peanut Butter has never been so affectionate. He aligns himself in front of Jelly and drapes his tail across Jelly's forehead. The boys circle. My legs are a maypole. They increase their speed. From my vantage point, they turn into one blurry, unending cat.

"They're going to spin themselves into butter," says Octavia.

Marjorie says, "Maybe Mom forgot to feed them."

Mags says, "No way. Her darlings?"

"Maybe she didn't feed them enough," Marjorie says under her breath.

Octavia says, "Maybe they're going to eat Mary."

The fact that my sister calls me by my real name shows me how scared she is.

I say, "They're fine, y'all. I'm fine."

I'm not sure what I should do to get out of the situation. Do I need to do anything? Won't the brothers tire themselves out? Lose interest? Their circling is strange, but cats do it all the time in cat food commercials. Their speed is off-putting, but they're not hurting me. My legs are warm, but the warmth isn't bad.

Marjorie and Mags move forward to wrangle their pets.

I say, "No, really, I'm fine."

But I'm not. The tingling is back. The fire ants have found me. They spool my calves and shins. I no longer care if my sister is scared because I want these cats off. If Peanut Butter and Jelly have done to me what the deli cat did, my legs will sprout fur from my ankles to kneecaps.

I inadvertently kick one of them in the ribs, eliciting a hushed *miaow*. A warning. The cats don't stop circling.

I reach down to separate them. That's when I get scratched.

I can see by my sister's face that what's happened is ugly. Funny: if Ling Ling had scratched me, Octavia wouldn't hesitate to scratch her right back. Scratch her bald-headed! Scratch her eyes out! Octavia has no fear of Ling Ling, Nightingale girls, or anyone meaner, bigger, or smarter than she is. But, *dang*, she is scared of Peanut Butter and Jelly. She flees down a long corridor toward the twins' rooms. I hear two doors slam as she barricades herself inside their shared bathroom.

"Peanut Butter!" Marjorie scoops him up and tosses him away from me. The cat lands on the hardwood and slides, spinning like the last legs of a top. He crashes into a receiving table. A cut glass vase topples. Drooping tulips are crushed, lithe green necks severed. Water spills and beads across the Pledge. The vase rolls, tulips twisting with it, onto the floor. The thud scares the bejeezus out of Peanut Butter, who jumps and cracks his head on the underside of table.

"Serves you right, you bad boy! Mary, are you okay?"

But it wasn't Peanut Butter who scratched my hand; it was Jelly. The cat sitting beside my ankle is licking my blood off his front paw. He's proud of himself. He spreads his toe pads and licks the hard-to-reach spots in between.

Mags grabs him. Marjorie grabs Peanut Butter. The twins aren't going to put up with their cats' rotten behavior anymore.

They grip the boys under their front legs and carry them at arms' distance. I follow them up the winding staircase that leads to a second-floor den and master bedroom. Mags nudges open her parents' door. She hurls Jelly across the room to land on the bed. Marjorie throws Peanut Butter after him. The cats tumble to the far side of the bedspread. I hear the material rip. The boys spring off the rumpled mess and, with midair twists, land to face us. They crouch. Their hackles rise, and their inkblot faces smolder. Their ice blue crossed eyes zone in on where I stand.

I glance down at my knee socks and am relieved to see that although the wool is tight from what has sprouted underneath, the fur is contained. The scratch across the back of my hand isn't bleeding badly. Amazingly enough, no fur has come out of the clotted red line. I blow cool air on the scratch.

The cats fly off the bed.

Mags slams the door. "Rabies!"

Marjorie says, "How? They never leave the house."

We race down the stairs to get away from a new blitz of crying. We hole up in Mags's room, but the crying comes through. Still locked in the bathroom, Octavia is nowhere to be seen.

"Maybe it's not as loud as we think," I say.

"Yeah, like a tree falling in a forest," Marjorie nervously agrees. "Maybe we hear it because we know that it's there."

Mags clicks on her flat screen, and we luck into a mind-numbing block of reruns from season one of *America's Next Top Model.* To drown out the cats, she raises the volume as high as it will go. The three of us line our backs against the single bed and draw the comforter over our legs. After several minutes, Octavia ventures out and plops herself into the over-sized beanbag chair.

Hours pass, and I decompress enough to soak in what's happening on-screen. But all the models remind me of Ling Ling. They're twice her height but, like Ling Ling, know how to walk across a room and command attention. I can see why Nick is drawn to her. I can see why dreadlocked, spike-haired, and tattoo-headed boys are also drawn to her. Those types would never give me a second look. Up until now, Nick has never looked my way either. What's his sudden interest in me?

Without thinking, I brush a hand over my socks from under the safety of the covers. Everywhere I squeeze, there is fur underneath. The fur is slick in some places, tangled in others. What is wrong with me? What's happening?

Kathryn Ann barges in. Home from broadcasting her show, her tight, surgically enhanced face is creased with anger. Hand on her hip, she says, "Please, ma'ams, will one of y'all kindly explain why my darlings are shut up in my room like it's a pound? Those boys have nearly put a hole through my door trying to claw their way out!"

chapter nine

It's close to midnight, and Marjorie and Mags have returned from their mother's room, where Kathryn Ann made them clean up the mess the cats made. Tasks included sweeping wood shavings off the floor, stripping the shredded bedspread and underlying sheets, bringing those sheets to the building's basement incinerator, remaking the bed, wiping cat pee off the walls, picking up knickknacks the boys had knocked off her vanity table, and super-gluing heads back onto two porcelain penguins from her collection.

Kathryn Ann hadn't analyzed the cats' behavior. She'd said to her daughters, "Animals are animals. It's not for us to reason why. But don't you dare shut them up like that again. You're lucky I'm not calling Mary and Octavia's parents."

Then, she'd sedated the boys. Kathryn Ann's antidrug campaign does not include prescribed medications because she can't get her nerve up to fly without generic Xanax or go to sleep without generic Ambien. She crushed half a pill of each and then mixed the powder in with the brothers' Fancy Feast. Currently, her darlings are conked out, curled head to toe, yin and yang, on top of her Eddie Bauer carry-on that's parked in the back of her walk-in closet. Kathryn Ann is laid out on top of her covers. The twins said she didn't bother to change into her pajamas; she just shed her skirt and suit jacket, then timbered onto the bed in her control tops. Thanks to her own regular nightly dosage, she'll sleep like a mummy.

The girls and I nuke Hot Pockets and play Truth or Dare. Hey, if I don't go along, they'll know something is wrong. As long as I don't touch my legs, I might be able to make it through the night without panicking. I can do it. I am not going home.

The Hot Pockets stink, so we stay in Mags's room. Marjorie won't allow food in hers because, to her nose, every odor lingers. I've seen her use a toothbrush to scrub spilled hot chocolate out of hairline cracks in the hardwood floor. She saved up her allowance to order a $49 broom off QVC. Mags encourages us to make a mess in her room because it drives her sister nuts.

Mags jokes, "Stains are proof that our friends love me best!"

Marjorie was given the bigger room because of her sleepwalking, but Mags got the terrace. The terrace wraps around the north and west sides of the penthouse. The twins' dad loves it. He's Eastern European and marvels at the sun like a Neanderthal. Although I've never seen him out there, evidence of his presence remains: Speedos slung over a cheap lounge chair; a hardback spy novel, pages warped from rain; and a fold-out aluminum face-tanner. The terrace is what makes this apartment worth tens of millions of dollars, but Kathryn Ann never sets foot onto it. What rich people on Fifth Avenue will never tell you is that their terraces are covered in pigeon poop.

Mags aims the water gun she uses to shoot the gray rats with wings at me. "Mary, truth or dare?"

Octavia has already been dared to go out on the icy terrace and pull the frosty, neon orange, banana hammock over her sweats. Marjorie was dared to take one of her mother's muscle relaxers but wouldn't unless her sister did too. Mags popped a pill but didn't have to be dared—so she opted for truth and revealed she'd been felt up by my neighborhood deli owner's son behind the potato chip rack.

This is scandalous on many fronts. None of us know the deli owner's son's name, he's nineteen, and he's opting out of college. He is constantly cleaning the deli and thus never seen without yellow rubber gloves, which most likely means he touched her boobs while wearing them.

I don't want to be asked why I've still got my school socks on under my flannel Hello Kitty pajamas, so I choose dare.

Mags says, "I dare you to call your boyfriend."

I shoot her a withering stare. "Nick's not my boyfriend. In case you forgot, he's Ling Ling's boyfriend."

Octavia says, "If he was her boyfriend, he's not anymore."

"Yeah," says Marjorie. "Turning your boyfriend over to the principal for drug possession is definitely grounds for a breakup."

Mags says, "I can't believe Nick and her were together."

"Nick and *she*," corrects her sister.

"Nick and *she*," mocks Mags. "And you wonder why you've never been kissed."

Along with Marjorie, both Octavia and I squirm at this remark. Besides Mags, none of us in this room has been kissed. We're not even sure Mags is telling the truth about the deli owner's son, but we want to believe her. Our lack of "experience" is ridiculous. We're sixteen. According to *Gossip Girl*, we should be on the pill.

Mags says, "You have to call him, Mary. It's a dare!"

I say, "I'm not getting star-sixty-nined."

"Nice try," Marjorie says, "You know very well you can't star-sixty-nine an unlisted number."

Mags passes me the portable and holds her water gun to my temple. "Put it on speaker."

I stare at the buttons "I don't know his number by heart."

This doesn't stop Mags. She scrolls through the digital redial listings. Last weekend, I accepted this same exact dare. We'd found Nick's home number in the Purser-Lilley sophomore class phone tree, and I'd called and listened to Nick's yiayia try to coax me into talking.

"*Ela!* Speak!" she had said.

I called back twice, hoping Nick would answer so I could listen to him say hello, breathe, then say hello one more time before hanging up. But every time, it was his yiayia.

"Nai?" The old woman had found the whole thing hilarious. "Oh, you again! 'Private Caller.' Ela! Speak!"

Mags shoves the phone in my face.

Tonight, Nick answers before the first ring finishes. This late, his grandparents must be in bed. "Yeah?" he says. Not *Hello*, as I'd imagined. Not like every other person in the world answers the phone.

I don't say anything. The dare was to call, not to talk. The phone lies face-up on the PB Teen pink and purple floral rug. We're sitting around it like a campfire. The speaker makes Nick's steady breath sound obscene.

Nick says, "I know it's you, Mary."

Blood drains out of my face. I reach to poke off the phone, but Octavia grabs my elbow. Her fingers dig into the sensitive flesh above my funny bone. I can't bend my arm. Tilting toward each other, we struggle. I wonder if Octavia will forever be grabbing my elbow to stop me from doing what she thinks that I shouldn't.

She mouths the word: *Talk*.

I stop struggling. My sister lets go of me. I dare myself to say: "How did you know it was me?"

Nick says, "I figured you'd call to apologize."

"Oh, my gosh, you're right. Detention! I'm so sorry. If I'd known it was yours, I'd never have gone in her locker."

I can't bring myself to say *marijuana* or *Ling Ling*, but the girls are doing their best impressions. Octavia's smoking an imaginary roach. Marjorie's made a makeshift bong with a can of her mother's Mississippi-imported Mello Yello. She's got a box of Goo Goo Clusters in her lap in preparation for the munchies. Mags has rolled her pajama bottoms up to her thighs, emptied a yellow shower caddy, and donned it upside down on her head. She's prancing around the same way our arch-nemesis did her laps in gym.

Nick says to me, "Yes, you would too have gone after it. You couldn't help yourself."

"What do you mean? I've never smoked in my life."

"You didn't find what you think you found."

"*What do you mean?* I saw it. Why would your grandparents say what they said? How could you let yourself get detention for nothing? Was it really just oregano?"

Octavia's lips freeze, pressed together; her thumb and first two fingers still pinch the figment of her imagination. Marjorie's make-believe lighter remains lit in front of the toxic green can. Mags removes the shower caddy, flips it, and holds it upright as if to collect information.

"It's not oregano," says Nick. "Or what my grandparents call oregano. But it is herbal. From Greece. My grandparents were covering for me with Principal Sheldon. If the government finds out about what it really is, they'll make it illegal."

"What is it?"

"Tell me first, how did it make you feel?"

"I didn't feel anything."

"You wouldn't have gone after it if it didn't make you feel good."

It's true. Before I knew what it was or where it was coming from, I knew I'd do anything for it. I'd imagined spreading it on the floor and rolling around on it like people in movies do on $100 bills. But who does that in real life? Money is filthy. To throw yourself at wrinkled, dirty paper, think of the kind of addict you'd have to be. Me. I don't want to admit this in front of the girls. I don't want to tell Nick he's right. Whatever is wrong with me can't be good.

I ask him, "How does it make Ling Ling feel?"

"Ling Ling never feels anything."

"So, why did you give it to her?"

"Honestly," his voice softens as if Ling Ling is listening in, "to get to you. To find out if you are what I think you are."

The girls' lips form Os. They bring their hands to their cheeks, and their fingers flutter as if they had a three-way tie for Miss Teen USA. They don't care if Nick is a drug pusher or another girl's boyfriend. He is talking on the phone with me, and he is saying what boys in our class never say.

I whisper, "What's so special about me all of a sudden?"

Nick says, "The turning."

The girls look confused.

He says confidential-like, "I know what you're going through."

Could Nick be talking about what's under my socks? Should I show the girls the fur? I can't. They'll shun me. Who wants to split Hot Pockets and share a comforter cover with someone who's turning? Turning must mean spoiling like milk does when it curdles. Milk gets fuzzy when it's old. Have I reached some sort of expiration date? Am I going bad? Is it written in my closed adoption papers that I have some rare Mediterranean genetic disorder? Does Nick mean to tell me that he's had encounters with cats that have left him with patches of fur that snap razors? But he did fall asleep under the parachute. Maybe he does know. Maybe he has the cure.

He says, "Tell me where you are. I'll help you."

"You want to help me right now in the middle of the night?"

No response. Not a further word out of him. I hear him breathing. I imagine being close enough to see that breath come out of his lips on a cold night like tonight. I wish we were together, but I'm deluding myself that he's got my same problems.

Nick asks, "Is it orange?"

I say, "I'm at Marjorie and Mags's apartment."

"Shush!" says Mags. Hold up, did she not hear what he said about me being orange? Has she also forgotten we're trying to hide that he's on speaker phone? She screams, "Nick, don't come!" Nope. She wants him to hear. "Nick, it's too late at night!"

"Our mom will kill us!" Marjorie joins in. "The doorman will call when you get here, and the phone will wake her up! She'll go ballistic!"

Octavia shouts, "Nick, listen to us, we're *screaming!* Come on over! Their mom's comatose!"

"But what if tomorrow, the doorman tells Mom that Nick was here?"

"Oh, my God, Mags, he'll totally tell her! Nick, you can't come. Don't!"

"Nick, don't you dare!"

"Nick? Nick?"

"Nick? Say something!"

The phone is dead. He's coming. He lives on 93rd and Fifth. At a fast clip, he'll be here in five minutes.

Mags flings her comforter back on her bed and plops two pillows at the headboard. She tosses the box of Goo Goo Clusters on her nightstand and tucks the water gun in the drawer.

Marjorie says, "Stop straightening—you're awful at it! You can't have him in your room. He's not coming into this apartment. Mary, go down to the lobby and wait for him. Act like you're going home."

Octavia says, "At this hour? In those clothes?"

I'm still in my Hello Kitty pajamas. I grab my book bag, with my school uniform stashed inside, and head for the bathroom.

Mags says, "What, Mary, you're Octavia—too embarrassed to change in front of us?"

I say, "Close your curtains."

"For what? We're too high up for anyone to see us from the street. Nobody on the other side of the park has their binoculars out."

Octavia says, "Let Gypsy Rose Lee change where she wants."

"It's fine," I say. "I'm fine." The sooner I get changed, the sooner I can go downstairs and meet Nick.

I take out my skirt and pull it over my pajama bottoms. The flannel against flannel has a clingy effect. The plaid pleats bunch up. I have to suck in my stomach to button the skirt over the pajamas' thick elastic waistband. I notice my reflection in the dark terrace windows. I look like a circus bear wearing a tutu.

Nick looks like the last time I saw him.

In the same athletic shorts and Purser-Lilley T-shirt he wore in the principal's office, Nick is standing barefoot on the terrace in front of Mag's glass door.

chapter ten

You'd think we'd scream, and we do.

Nick's arms are crossed to ward off the cold. His head is tucked into his throat. His curly black hair blows toward us. His curls cover his eyes. The winter wind is so fast and so strong that it rattles the glass terrace door in the frame. When I push the door open, Nick weaves out of the way, but he doesn't come in.

He lifts his head.

His eyes are deepened and darkened by pupils dilated by the night to leave only an outline of brown. His lips are crimsoned but not cracked by the cold. He extends a hand, the palm of which is as dirty as I imagine the soles of his bare feet to be.

Mags says to him, "Are you crazy? Nobody's coming out there with you!"

Octavia says, "He wants Mary."

"I know, but it's freezing outside. And now it's freezing in here! Nick, get in so we can shut the door."

I ask him, "How did you get up here? The fire escape? Why?"

Nick doesn't answer me, so why ask him about his clothes— or lack thereof? He knows what he's got on: a whole lot of nothing. His bare arm remains stretched toward me. He looks right at me as if my sister and the twins are not here.

The room is flushed with icy air. Marjorie's teeth chatter, and she buzzes to make the chattering more pronounced. She wants me to hurry and make a choice. Am I in, or am I going out? I'm too frigid to budge. I'm stunned: at the temperature, at Nick's strange tolerance of it, his unorthodox arrival, his intensity. I'm embarrassed. Even though I'm wearing my pajama bottoms, my skirt is whipping around my hips in the wind.

Nick speaks, and I see the clouds of his warm breath I'd imagined being close to. "Come out. I'll explain everything."

I'll explain everything is what guilty people say in the movies. Usually, they are standing over a dead body or are with someone other than their spouse in their marital bed. You say it to someone you don't want to disappoint. You have a history with that person and you don't want that history to end. But Nick and I have never spoken until today. As Kathryn Ann would say about Nick, *I don't know him from Adam.* Nobody else in Mags's room knows Nick that well either.

Behind him, the warped pages of the spy novel flap on the lounge chair. A gust of wind swoops the open book up and off the roof like a bird. The Speedo is swept into a neon orange ball in the corner. What if the wind takes me too? The terrace lights aren't lit. What if I step on something sharp, cut my foot wide open, and have to get stitches? What if a pigeon flies into my hair? What if there is a blanket of mice? What if? What if? What if! What if a boy never again scales the side of a building to see me? I take Nick's dirty hand and follow him into the night.

None of the girls stops me.

Octavia takes hold of the terrace doorknob to close it. As she struggles with the door's heft against a rush of wind, Mags flicks off her bedroom lights as if she's giving us privacy—but I know it's really so they can spy on us without being seen. Marjorie yanks Mags's comforter off the bed, squeezes past Octavia, and tosses it over my shoulders. As the terrace door shuts, I hear Mags shout at her sister through the glass.

"Hey! That's my comforter! It's gross out there. It's gonna get stained. What am I going to sleep under?"

"What do you care, slob? We'll sleep in my room."

Marjorie and Octavia drag Mags through the twins' shared bathroom to Marjorie's side. I don't overhear anything else from them. Mags's bedroom lights remain out.

I can't read Nick's face because my eyes haven't adjusted to the loss of light from the apartment. I'm floating with him again—but this time in blackness. Despite the comforter, pajamas, wool skirt, and socks, the spot where his hand is connected to mine is the warmest part of my body. He lets go. My hand is instantly colder.

The wind shoves me, and I worry I might tip over. I hug the comforter around my chest. I sense Nick move behind me. He lays his hands on my shoulders. He guides me to the lounge chair, where he sits and sinks into the plastic weave. Then, he pulls me into the cavern of his spread arms and legs.

Nick doesn't get under the comforter with me. He holds me like I'm sitting upright in a sleeping bag. There is a fat, fluffy layer of feathers sewn into squares between my back and his chest. I am swaddled to my neck. Nick's arms keep the comforter closed in front of my body. I hold my own hands.

I ask, "How are you not freezing to death?"

Nick presses his palms into the comforter. My belly grows warm under the pressure. He says, "That's part of what I have to explain."

"The turning?"

He rests his chin on my right shoulder. That spot grows warm too, and the warmth radiates up my neck, ending at my earlobe with a gentle pinch. This must be what it's like to have my ear nibbled. Over the edge of the cement-brick wall of the terrace, skeletal treetops stretch from Fifth Avenue across Central Park to the West Side. Snow clings to rickety branches. If I weren't so nervous, I might consider it beautiful.

Nick says, "I want to be with you when it happens. When it happened to me last summer, I was alone in Greece with my grandparents. They were in their garden, getting high with their friends. I was supposed to be taking an afternoon siesta. But I couldn't sleep and then I thought I was dying."

"I'm going to feel like I'm dying?"

"It doesn't feel good."

"What's *it*?"

"I could smell it on you at school—probably before you knew anything was wrong. Well, not *wrong*. Different? Special? *Kala?* Yiayia and Papou have words in two languages to avoid saying there's anything wrong with their only grandson. Doctors don't recognize it, so everything we use to deal with it is herbal. My grandparents are cool about sharing their pot, and we go to Naxos every summer to score *nip*."

"Nip?"

"What you found in her bag. Nip brings the turning out of you. Pot slows it down."

Nip, pot, the turning—I'm not even listening. All I heard was a hole: Nick didn't say Ling Ling's name.

I ask, "Your folks are okay with this?"

"My parents don't know. Yiayia says if Mom found out, she'd send me for all kinds of medical tests. She says I'll outgrow it. It's a phase. She's never heard of it lasting more than five years. It's more common in Greece but still believed to be myth."

"Like Zeus?"

"No, not like Zeus. The turning is real."

"So, I *am* sick."

He gives me a squeeze, and I am oddly comforted, electrified, and frightened at the same time. He says, "I wouldn't say sick. I mean, you wouldn't think of a gay dude's gayness as sick. It's seasonal. Two weeks in January and then most of the summer. You can't totally suppress it, no matter how much you smoke.

You have to let it out if you want to be normal most of the time. I can make it easier for you."

I nod again, having no idea what Nick is talking about.

It's like when my parents talked to Octavia and me about sex when we were kids. They were never specific. They talked of love but not mechanics. If we wanted details, Dad would say, "Ask your mother." Mom would say, "Look it up in the dictionary." That's how I learned that the word Ben Strong called a mean kid in the third grade is slang for *the male organ of copulation*, which means *to engage in intercourse*, which means *physical contact between individuals that involves the genitalia,* which brought me back to the first word I looked up. "Round and round," Mom said, "that's pretty much how it goes.*"

Nick says, "New York is dangerous for people like us. Very territorial. Very us-against-them. If they find out about you, they'll make you pick sides."

"What sides? Who are *they*?"

Nick unwraps an arm and points. "That's they."

From the fire escape, a body is lumbering over the terrace wall. The figure's limbs are long and lanky. I can't distinguish thighs from calves or forearms from biceps. Like Nick, the figure is dressed in shorts and a T-shirt. The shorts are cutoffs. Closing in on us, his vintage 1980s iron-on reads: *I'm the boss, Applesauce!* His toenails are painted black. He's wearing yellow dishwashing gloves. The same pair that supposedly squeaked around under Mags's shirt. He is the deli owner's son.

"Yoon." Nick calls him by name. He draws me closer. "You couldn't let me do this alone?"

Yoon pokes the end of our lounge chair with his foot, jostles us.

Nick sounds wary. "Dude, seriously. Go."

Yoon spies the collar of my cartoon pajamas peeking out from my comforter cocoon. He smirks the smirk of a smartass. Like any smartass, he can't keep a snide comment to himself. His voice is baritone, slow like a yawn.

"Hello, Kitty."

He hooks his arms around my knees and yanks me out of Nick's tight hold.

I land on my spine. The comforter softens the impact, but pain sears a line from my neck to my tailbone. The cement is covered with dead leaves and dirty snow-water. The air is mildewed. There is a wet rustling as Nick lunges over me and tackles Yoon.

The boys roll across the terrace. Yoon's legs are a vise around Nick's thighs. Nick bear-hugs Yoon's chest, pinning his arms. Yoon rears back his head and swings his gaping mouth into Nick's throat. Nick releases him. He bats Yoon's face with loose fists. The boys scramble apart, get to their feet, lunge at each other, and roll again.

I want to scream for help, but the fire ants have found me. They crawl up and out of my knee socks and take over every bit of my flesh. They are between my toes, behind my ears, and in every crevice in between. They scamper across my scalp. They bite. Their bites are unbearable. I twist and scratch inside the suffocating comforter. I'm trapped.

The boys lean over me, say things—to me, to each other—I can't make out. My hearing is fading. I'm shrinking. The boys' faces get bigger and rise like moons.

Yoon blinks. When his eyes close, they are chestnut. Open, they are emerald green. He smiles, parts his teeth, and unrolls a long, narrow pink tongue. He licks the tips of his incisors, which have grown past his lower gums to form fine points.

He purrs, his voice velvet. And that's when he says what he says about us not being vampires.

And then it happens...

chapter eleven

Yoon's tongue is long and sandpapery. It curls under my chin, swipes the side of my face, wipes goo out of the corners of my eyes, and then goes into my ear. It tickles. I want more of it, even though I am not sure what just happened or how I got myself into a position to be licked—especially by the deli owner's son. My school skirt, knee socks, and pajamas are in a pile on the terrace. Yoon's shorts, T-shirt, and yellow gloves are piled alongside.

I remember.

Emerald eyes. Black mask. Copper face. White mouth. A blur of teeth and fur. A cannonball made out of cotton. Yoon has turned into the deli cat.

And I have turned into a kitten.

I wriggle away from Yoon but am cupped in Nick's human hands.

Yoon is sitting on Nick's lap while Nick offers me to him for a bath.

Nick says something to me I can't understand. English is foreign. He could speak Greek, and I'd understand it the same. He is using a soothing tone, saying my name a lot because it's the one word I recognize. "*Mary*, (fill in the blank with information on my officially turning). *Mary*, (fill in the blank with bullshit about how everything is going to be okay). *Mary*, (I'll learn to live with it). *Mary*, (insert what he previously alluded to about medicinal herbs and us versus them)."

Yoon nibbles my neck. There is a tangle in the fur, and he tugs it loose with his teeth. He tugs too hard, and I squeak. My mew is minuscule. I could cry out with all my might, and Octavia and the twins wouldn't hear me. If I turn back into a girl—*pleasepleaseplease, let me turn back into a girl!*—I promise myself that I will be louder in school. Louder in life. I'll use an "outside voice" inside. To be heard, I'll need practice.

"Mew!"

Nick hears me. He grabs Yoon by the throat and shoves him. Yoon plunges backward into the plastic weave of the lounge chair. He bounces up, squirms, and rights himself, but a furry hind leg slips through two plastic strips. He jerks it free, gains his balance by placing his four feet wide apart on the aluminum frame. He sports the same perturbed look he had on when he straddled my open toilet.

Nick has stayed human to make sure Yoon doesn't pick me up by the scruff of my neck and carry me off to his lair behind the potato chip rack. He places me in the cradle of his bare thighs. If I turn back into a girl—*pleasepleaseplease*—I am copping a feel.

Settling onto my belly, I place my arms (no, my *front legs*) one on top of the other an inch below Nick's shorts. I flex my hands (no, my *paws*), and nails (no, *claws*) come out. In real life (I mean, *human* life), my fingernails are short because they're always in my mouth. I marvel at the length, sharpness, and translucency of my claws. I press them into Nick's flesh to test them. Nick clenches his thighs, and I rise an inch. I retract my claws, grateful I possess weapons that will serve me while my voice is weak.

In between my hind legs, fit snugly together, is a tail. I have a tail: muscles and a length of bone I've never used. It might as well be pinned on like a paper donkey's. It lies limp because I don't know what to do with it. When Yoon licks the tip, it involuntarily flicks.

Nick strokes between my ears with one finger. My ears! They're no longer on the sides of my head—they're on top. The space between them is so small that there is room for only two of Nick's fingers. He switches to two. He rubs the top of my head. He rubs his thumb under my chin. Above and below my face, there is heavenly petting. Nick could crush my skull if he wanted. But I trust him—just like that. Animal instinct.

I'm not as quick to judge Yoon. His tongue on my tail makes my hind legs twitch. He's had his own tail licked and knows how to lick mine. Whether he's cleaning or kissing, his attention is manipulative: press this button and get the desired, expected response. I've never had my buttons pressed, but I decide Yoon can press all he wants. My kitten brain does not have room for language, so it stands to reason that it doesn't have room for a conscience. So what if Yoon's intentions aren't honorable? Who cares if I lose Mags's friendship because I let the guy (well, he's not really the same *guy*) she says she fooled around with fool around with me? Two boys at once? Call me what you want. I do not care. I give myself over to them and vibrate with pleasure.

Nick taps my front paw. Interpretation: pay attention. Tap, tap: focus. He is saying something about the color of my fur because after he taps my paw, he points to the neon orange Speedo glowing in a terrace corner. I'm not nearly as bright, but get the gist: orange is special. Nick looks like he's never seen my color before. He's looking at me in what must be the same way the twins' dad looks at the sun.

Yoon doesn't communicate with me via catspeak or mental telepathy. His purrs sound like purrs—they don't translate to words. I don't hear his velvet, human voice inside my head. He tells me what he wants with his actions.

He wants my fur spotless. He licks up my tail to my hip. His tongue searches for and removes bits of debris that will tarnish my coloring. Yoon is twenty pounds, while I doubt I'm even two. If he sinks his teeth into my throat, he'll rip it out before Nick stops him. If he swings his meaty paw at my head, he'll break my neck. But Yoon just licks, licks, licks. Who knew that the deli owner's bitter disappointment of a son was such a mama cat?

Nick pinches the air with his thumb and forefinger. I get it:

I won't be a kitten for much longer. He puts his hands in front of his face like parenthesis and blows up an imaginary balloon. With each breath, his hands spread farther apart. He slaps his hands together. Interpretation: when I turn back into a girl, it is going to be quick.

And here I go.

The fire ants are *under* my skin and then *inside* my bones. The ants are big and getting bigger. They want out of my body. They want my body to grow.

Nick spreads Mags's comforter on the terrace. He holds me with one hand. His fingers align under my ribs. I go limp. My legs hang over his thumb and pinky. His touch, as gentle as it may be intended, is too much. My body feels bruised.

"Mew!"

I can't hear myself over the wind. My head is pounding. I'm too weak to lift it. Nick places me on a comforter square.

Yoon crawls on top of me. He doesn't drop his weight but hovers. His bent legs are a cage. He cranes his head under his chest and gives my nose a lick.

My paws shake. They swell to the size of my kitten head. They blow up to the size of my human hands, but my paws are still paws—and then the fur splits apart. My skin shows through: kitten skin, not girl's. The kitten skin is pastier, textured like suede. Each strand of fur stiffens, stands on end like a porcupine's quills, and then sinks into my flesh with a thousand tiny stabs.

Yoon coaxes my human hands out of their padded shells. Under his tongue, round toe pads elongate to fingers. Knuckles emerge. The bone growth is torture. But Yoon continues to apply pressure, his tongue saying, *Easy does it. Easy...easy.* My hands feel sunburned. My kitten skin melts back to my own, caramelizing to my human color like sugar in a pan. There's the freckle that dots that back of my right pinky! I am so relieved to see the distinguishing mark (the one my mystery-writer mom jokes that she'll use to identify me if my severed hand is mailed to her by a serial killer), I almost overlook the orange fur that cuffs my wrists. That fur still covers the rest of me. My arms, torso, legs, feet, and every feature of my face must also return to normal. At the thought of the pain, I black out.

When I come to, I'm naked.

chapter twelve

Nick says, "Don't worry, we didn't see anything."

I'm on the terrace floor, wrapped in Mags's comforter. "And when you turned before, you turned in your pajamas. You were so small, you crawled out your pajama leg."

He helps me onto the lounge chair, but I don't need help. Although my movements are limited in this goose-down burrito (made heavier by the snow puddle I've been lying in), I am invigorated. I want to repel down the side of the building. Run through the park. Climb trees! Chase squirrels and steal their nuts!

I sit and rock, gripping the comforter in front of my bare breasts. I'm not cold. I'm feverish. But the fever feels good. I rub my calves together. The fur is gone. I feel my own silky, albeit stubbly, skin. I don't need a stitch of clothing to stay warm. I fight the urge to hop to my feet and flash Nick.

Sitting beside me, he pats my back.

"I'm calm." I tell him what he wants to hear. Back-patting is international for *There, there. Get a hold of yourself. Excitement's over.* I look around for Yoon.

I find him sleeping under the foot of the lounge chair. Yoon has not returned to boy form. His emerald eyes are shut, the lids camouflaged within his black mask. His mouth is curled up at the corners in a satisfied smile. He's on his back, which is broad enough for him to lay flat and keep him from toppling to either side. His front legs are bent, black paws loosey-goosey in the air. His hind legs hang open. His copper belly and balls are exposed. Yoon looks unbothered by his vulnerability. If I looked like him when I fell asleep in public, I might do it more often.

Nick says, "He's exhausted from helping you."

"I thought *you* were going to help me."

"I am. I did. What, you wish it was my tongue all over you?"

Good lord, the thought of it. I can barely bring myself to speak—but I do. "You think Ling Ling would like that?"

"I don't care what she likes."

I venture farther. "Are you two not together anymore?"

He leans his shoulder against mine—a nudge. Don't I get it? Temple to temple, his windblown curls tickle my eyebrow. Our warmness mingles. He slips his hand inside my comforter and fishes out my hand. He laces his fingers between mine. That's a good enough answer for me.

I ask, "Yoon's too tired to change?"

"Nah, he just prefers it this way."

"Why don't you?"

"Because I have to go to school. If I don't show up, my folks will find out. I'll get expelled, not detention. If I turn at night, I won't sleep. My grades will suck. Or, like Yoon, if I turn too much, I won't be able to stop myself from sleeping. It's like passing out wasted. You could wake up anywhere, but be bare-ass—"

"Naked." I finish his sentence. I squeeze his hand. I'm not embarrassed, and I don't know why.

Nicks says, "I have this theory that the less I turn, the shorter this *phase*, as Yiayia calls it, will last. When it ends, I want a normal life. To have that, I have to make it through Purser-Lilley, then college, and then I can start living for real. Yoon thinks this is the life. He's skipping college so he can turn as much as he wants. That's why he's always got those rubber gloves on. If you turn too much, there are side effects."

"I thought you said turning's two weeks, then the summer."

"It is, but Yoon always tries to make it last a little longer. Now that he's out of school, he can spend all his free time researching. There's hardly anything written about what we've got, but he keeps looking. He's always online or in the field."

"Yoon's parents don't know either?"

"Oh, they know. And they are not happy about the college deferment. But in Korea, his parents say what we have is seen as a gift. If Yoon went there, they say he'd be treated like a god, but his parents refuse to go back for political reasons. If Yoon wants to go on his own, he has to work to save the money, and his folks don't pay him much. He breaks a pickle jar, and they deduct it from his pay. They don't want him to go because they think he'll never come back. So, while he's here, they put up with his shit. No college, late nights running around, feeding strays in the back of their store. Yoon wants to be the first of our kind to be able to turn in his thirties. But that's sad."

"Sad how?"

"Sad pathetic. Like all those Purser-Lilley moms wearing low-rise skinny jeans. Oh, sorry, is your mom one of those?"

"No, she's pretty modest."

"My mom's clinging to her youth. Every time she sits down, I have to look away from her G-string. She says she's *European*, but that's code for exhibitionist. Do you know how mortifying it is to go to the beach in Greece with your mom?"

"No, but when we go to Myrtle Beach, my mom wears a huge hat and is always lecturing us to put on more sunscreen."

"Beaches in Greece are topless."

"Got it."

"So, forgive me if I don't want to embrace my wild side. Wild people embarrass themselves."

I think about that. The wildest thing I've ever done was going down a fifteen-story-high, spiral water-park tube last summer. A hundred and fifty twisty yards in one minute. My back bumped the fiberglass connector joints the whole way. My neck killed from straining to keep my head up. I was so scared of getting water up my nose, I held my breath. I didn't even scream. My face must have been blue when I shot out. It was a horrible rush—but it was a rush. The lifeguard gave me his hand, I tugged my one-piece out of my butt, and for the next half-hour, I thought I could do anything.

I could do anything now.

I kiss Nick—just take my temple off his and turn my lips to meet his mouth. He tenses, like when I pricked his bare thighs with my kitty claws, but I don't pull back. He could push me away if he wanted me to stop. He doesn't. He keeps hold of my hand and keeps his lips softly pressed against mine. It is black-and-white movie kissing: sweet, like I'd hoped.

Yoon mewls. He is dreaming of a meadow. His front paws bat at a butterfly. With a dream-leap, his body wrenches into a C. His heart races under his coarse copper chest. I let go of Nick's hand and reach for Yoon's belly. I want to rub it and reassure him, *You'll get that butterfly next time.*

Nick stops me. He says, "Don't get yourself started."

"If I touch him, I'll turn?"

"Yeah."

I touch my lips, tingling from Nick's kiss. I can't hide my panic. Are those warning tingles or tingles everybody gets when they kiss their crush?

Nick says, "Don't worry. Only touching a cat or one of us in cat form will trigger the turning. Soon enough, you'll learn to control it. I can. So can Yoon. Pot helps, and there are other ways. But for now, for you, the turning's like puberty. No matter what you do, zits happen."

For an idiotically vain moment, I'm grateful that I don't have any pimples.

He grins. "I'm normal now—kiss me as much as you want."

I do. He opens his mouth, and mine goes along. This is Technicolor kissing. He pulls me into his chest so that half my rear end is off the lounge chair. Wind sweeps between our bodies and into an open flap in my comforter cover.

Yoon miaows—a warning like the one I heard from Peanut Butter or Jelly when I put my foot through their spinning circle of a wagon train.

I ask, my lips barely lifting off Nick's, "Should we wake him? He sounds like he's having a nightmare."

"Let him have it," Nick mutters as he moves his mouth to my neck. His curls caress my throat. "Maybe he'll fall off a building and die in his sleep."

"Mrowl!" Yoon's warrior cry breaks us up. He is out from under the lounge chair. His lips retract. Drool drips off his canines.

"Back off, dude," Nick warns.

"What is it between you two?" I ask.

Nick says, "He doesn't want me this close to you. He thinks I'll talk you into suppressing the turning. If it was up to him, you'd turn all the time."

Yoon pounces at me.

Nick puts himself between us. Yoon hits Nick's chest. Nick falls backward into me. We all fall off the lounge chair. Caught in Nick's arms, Yoon's glowing emerald eyes implore me: *Help! He's bigger than me! Be on my side!* But Yoon looks plenty tough. Besides, what's a fair fight between a boy and a cat?

Nick gets to his feet. Yoon twists to free himself, but Nick chucks him in the air and then catches him like a bristled, saber-toothed sack of potatoes. Yoon sinks his claws into the curve of Nick's neck and shoulders. Nick curses. Dots of blood seep through his white Purser-Lilley T-shirt. Nick lifts Yoon straight up. His claws—wet with blood—slip out of Nick's skin and shirt. The fabric rips from an extra-long thumb claw. Yoon's black mask furrows.

Nick tosses him away from his chest like a basketball. Yoon rebounds off the terrace wall, lands on his feet, and gives his silent hiss. Yesterday, Yoon's no-noise made a battalion of mice scatter off my back landing, but tonight, it doesn't scare Nick.

Nicks stomps. *Scat!*

Yoon leaps onto the terrace wall and then dives off.

I run to the wall and lean over. I hear him before I spot him leaping from one grated fire-escape landing to the one below. He soars over the metal stairs. His copper coat blends with rust, but he becomes more visible in the light cast from the apartment lobby when he jumps to the sidewalk. I lose sight of him when he dashes across the tarred pavement to the bricked, Fifth Avenue border of Central Park and then into the bushes and trees.

Nick says, "I have to go after him. If I don't, he'll come back for you."

"So go."

"I can't catch him unless I turn."

"So turn."

"I don't want you to see."

"You saw me."

"That was different. Go inside."

"No."

"Go inside!"

"You can't make me."

When he kisses me, I think he can make me do whatever he wants.

But I want to see him turn! I tell myself to stop kissing him. Coach told us that smart girls like us get pregnant because they think only a boy can bring them to, as Webster's defines, *intense or paroxysmal excitement*, which means *an explosive discharge of neuromuscular tensions*. I close my eyes. His arms wind around me. One hand clutches the back of my neck. The other flattens against the small of my back. I want to let go of the comforter cover and let it drop to my ankles.

But my fingers won't open. They are clutching the comforter and will not unclutch. I want to slide my thigh between his legs, but my leg will not move. My head is locked. My jaw is locked open. My tongue is petrified against the roof of my mouth. My pulse throbs in my ears, but my chest won't rise or fall. My lungs are not filling with air.

Wait a second.

I am not breathing.

Nick steps away, and I stay stuck.

My eyelids are sealed shut, but wind fills my gaping mouth. Wind whips in the opposite direction, blowing my hair in front of my face. When the wind whips back, I can't shake my head to loosen stray strands caught in the moisture Nick has left on my lips.

I am paralyzed. I try to wiggle my fingers and toes, to unglue my eyes. Nothing works. Paralyzed is paralyzed—except my skin is alive! I feel everything. The ice-cold air against my exposed face, neck, and shoulders is electric. I should fight my paralysis, but it feels too good. My resolve is weakening because there is no air getting to my brain.

Nick says, "I'm sorry, Mary. You're not hurt. I only stole it for a minute—enough for me to turn and get away."

Breath-stealing? It's not a myth! What else cool can I do?

The comforter tugs between my hands. Nick must have dropped into cat form and landed on the hem. There's another tug as he kicks off. I hear his claws graze the top of the terrace wall. The fire escape clanks. The clanks grow more distant and then the sound of him fades into the sounds of the night.

My fingers crack as my hands unclench. My toes pop as I rise off my heels to flex my calves. I snap my neck, roll my head around in a circle. I hear a spark like when you touch a doorknob after walking across a carpeted room in your socks. It is the sound of a breath: mine.

I open my eyes and inhale more deeply. I am alone but still buzzed. I can move, but I don't. I remain on the terrace, gazing out over the trees, and feel what's left of the good feeling Nick gave me until it is gone.

chapter thirteen

On the far side of Mags's pitch-black room, Octavia sits in the oversized beanbag chair. She holds Kathryn Ann's box of Goo Goo Clusters. She plucks out a foil-wrapped, chocolate hockey puck and throws it at my face.

I duck.

The Goo Goo smacks the glass door. I dodge the next one before it's out of her hand. She tries to pelt me with Goo Goo after Goo Goo, but I am too quick. I stand in place, clad in Mags's down comforter, and bob left and right. I see everything that's thrown. To my new eyes, the room is bright.

Out of ammunition, Octavia throws the box.

She scrambles out of the beanbag. The bag is slippery. It scrunches when she shoves her hands into the blob. She reaches for the edge of the nightstand and pulls herself up. She sweeps her hands across the front of the table, slides open the drawer, and grasps for Mags's water gun. She aims it at me like a Smith & Wesson.

She says, "I can't live with you like this."

"Like what?"

"Don't even try it. I saw what you are."

"What did you see?"

"Mary, don't. I saw you. *You know* what I saw!"

"Did the twins see?"

"Does it matter? I saw. I can't live with you! Mom and Dad won't understand. They'll think I'm crazy. I'll be put in a state home and then out on my ass at eighteen!" The water gun shakes in her hands. She whimpers, "My life is over."

"Octavia, did the twins see?" I beg to know.

"No!"

"Are you sure?"

"What difference does it make? You turned. Into. A cat! Your boyfriend turned into a cat! And so did that deli guy!"

"Yoon."

"Whoever!" Her eyes are wide and misty. "They gave you cat! You caught cat!"

I tug the comforter around my shoulders and wait for an answer to my question about the twins seeing or not seeing. I could stand with my back against the terrace door and wait like this all night. I am eerily calm. It's like I've taken one of Kathryn Ann's airplane pills. *Oh, my word, y'all, is that turbulence? Well, that is just fine. Oh, my word, y'all, are we nose diving? Well, that is fine too. Tailspin? Hon, would you mind unhooking yourself from that jump seat and getting me a splash more Tabasco sauce for this here tomato juice?*

Octavia says, "Look at you—you're all stalker-y, like a cat. Fine!" She nods to the twins' closed communal bathroom door. "They tried waiting up for you, but the Xanax took effect. They're doped up like Peanut Butter and Jelly. Oh, God, Mary, I hate those cats, and now I'll have to hate you."

"You don't hate Peanut Butter and Jelly," I tell her. "You're scared."

"Hell, yes, I'm scared! Of you! How can you be so reasonable? You are standing in front of me in a comforter with your clothes in your hands—with two different boys' clothes in your hands! You're talking to me like we're talking about you breaking curfew. You turned. Into. A cat!"

"What did Nick look like?"

"A frickin' cat!"

"What kind?"

"I don't know! I was trying not to look. Besides, all cats look alike—"

"In the dark."

"Don't play with me, Mary." She is serious; she wouldn't call me by my name otherwise. "I hate cats. All cats. They're disgusting, selfish, nasty. Vicious!"

"Peanut Butter and Jelly?"

"Yes! Is your memory that short?"

I raise my hand to examine Jelly's scratch, but the cut is gone. A faint line is all that's left of the crusty scab from a few hours ago. Along with unabashed boy-kissing, breath-stealing, and in-the-dark seeing, quick healing must be something else the post-cat me can do. I study the tips of my normally bitten-to-the-quick fingers. My fingernails are short but not ragged. There's not one hangnail. Every cuticle is smooth.

I offer my hand to Octavia for her to inspect, but she trembles twenty feet away against the wall. She brandishes the water gun. She doesn't want me to leave my spot against the terrace door. We're alone in a room together. I am breaking her cardinal cat phobia rule.

I say, "I'm not going to hurt you."

"Yes, you will. You can't help it. Cats are hunters."

"I'm not a hunter."

"You are, whether you know it yet or not!"

"What do you think I'm going to do, chase you under the bed? Pick you up with my mouth?"

"You'll give me a heart attack."

"You're sixteen."

"So, you'll *scare* me to death! I'm not debating you. You turned. Into. A cat!"

I take a step. My front foot hasn't touched the floor, but Octavia hears the rustle of the comforter.

She fires.

Streams of water splat the cover. Water hits my hands. Water strikes my throat, shoulders, and face. It clings to my flesh as if my flesh were fur. My face is slick and slimy, as if I bobbed for pepperoni on an extra-large pizza.

The gun clicks. The tip drips. Octavia sucks out what's

left in the barrel. Her thirst sated, she grabs Marjorie's $49 broom.

"*You're* the hunter!" I shout at her.

She holds the bristled end toward me. "I'm sorry. I can't let you near me."

But I want to get near her. I am drenched, and now that she knows about what's happening to me, she should be offering me her sisterly help. I'm gonna get that broom.

I lunge. She swats me. I go after her. She swats me harder, many more times, until I'm running from her. I jump on the bed, she swats me off. I jump on the beanbag, she swats me toward the desk. I hop on the edge, land on my butt, pivot off. Her broom knocks over the desk chair. I hopscotch over strewn Goo Goo Clusters, but Octavia steps on them. The foil packages pop. Caramel, marshmallow, and peanuts squish between her toes and slow her down. I shimmy into Mags's closet that's too messy to close. I press my back against the wall and hug the relatively few hung clothes to my chest. My arms sting where Octavia swiped me. I glance along the outside lengths of my legs and see what feels like razor burn there too.

Octavia says, "Girl, don't you know that you're nekkid?"

I peer out of the closet. Mags's comforter is stuck in the door.

Truth be told, I did know. But being naked felt natural. It feels natural now.

I say, "Looks like my days of self-consciousness are over. Whatever's happening to me can't be all bad. No more changing clothes under other clothes! Try it. You might like it. You could stop getting dressed in your bunk and showering by yourself after gym. Maybe we should see how shy you are if I bite you!"

Octavia jabs me with the broom handle. She kicks Mags's mound of shoes and clothes into the closet. She tries to shove the door closed to trap me.

"I'm not gonna bite you!" I say. "Besides, I don't think that's how it works. I think you're born with it. So, if Mom and Dad are sending anyone back to foster care, it's me. I'm the one with the problem."

Octavia sniffs. Her voice is shaky. "Your problem is real—mine's in my head. Head cases always lose to medical conditions."

"You know, Mom and Dad don't have to know about either of us. I'm not going to tell if you don't. You said you saw me." I try to get a smile out of her. "How can you be scared of a pwecious widdle kidden?"

Octavia's lips tighten.

She says, "Kittens cry all the time. They get their heads stuck in glasses and bags. They hide in sofa cracks. You sit on them or knock them across the room when you open a door. When you step on their tails, they make the worst sound."

I hear something in her voice I've never heard before. I ask, "How do you know?"

"My last foster mom was a cat-hoarder."

"A what?"

"One of those women who has a hundred cats." Her shoulders slump. The fight has gone out of her.

"You're exaggerating," I soothe.

"Okay, Oprah, she had forty-five cats. She was old. She couldn't climb the stairs to my room, which was an attic, by the way, but the cats could get up there. I could never get them all out. There was always one under the bed, or behind a curtain, or on a shelf in the closet, or under a pillow. They pissed on the wallpaper and shit in corners because she forgot to change their litter boxes. Her eyes were milked-over, her nose was shot. The house should have been condemned."

"I can't believe child services put you there to begin with."

"As long as you don't kill anyone, they'll keep the checks and kids coming."

"Why didn't you say anything?"

"What was I supposed to say? To who? I was seven, and my parents were dead. My brother and sisters wouldn't take me. I'd been through other foster parents. The old woman didn't hit me. She loved those cats, even though she couldn't take care of them. I figured I had no right to complain."

"But it was—"

"Hell," Octavia says. "Some were sick. Skinny. Spines showing through. Shit stuck in their paws because they were too sick to bathe. They'd cough up hair balls, puke. That vomit noise…chug, chug, chug, CHWACK! I hate it. They'd chase each other across the furniture. Stuffing hung out from where they sharpened their claws. There was no place to sit where you wouldn't sit on a spring or get run over. I couldn't eat a bowl of cereal without them crawling all over me because they wanted the milk."

"Why didn't she stop them? You were her kid—they were animals."

"Those cats were her *darlings*, like Peanut Butter and Jelly are Kathryn Ann's. The old lady made me put my cereal on the floor as soon as I was finished. So many cats would crowd around that bowl, it would disappear. At night, they'd crowd around me, and *I* would disappear. They'd dive-bomb me. Attack my feet under the sheets. Blow in my face. Chew, rip out my hair. They covered me like my milk bowl. I fought but never won."

"How come you never told me?"

Octavia props the broom against the closet hanging rod. I could take hold of it, but I'm too stunned to move as she raises her pajama top. She trusts me enough to turn her back.

I see.

Her skin is crisscrossed with slim, raised, overlapping welts: cat scratches. Hundreds of them. From when she couldn't fight and curled up like a ball. That's why she won't change clothes in front of me. Eight years of sharing the same room, and I never knew.

I whisper, "No wonder you hate me."

"I don't hate you. I love you. You're my sister. But I can't live with a cat again."

• • •

At six-thirty, the sun isn't up, but we get dressed. My school skirt is hot and stiff and smells like the Purser-Lilley indoor water ballet aquatics center from spending the night draped on the radiator. I steal a pair of Mags's navy knee socks because she'll never miss them. I stuff Nick's and Yoon's clothes in my backpack.

Octavia leaves a note excusing our early departure, claiming she wants to get a jump-start on prep for the upcoming debate against Dalton. She writes that she wants to be the first one into The Cellar Used Bookstore (her never-fail research trove) when it opens at eight. She needs me to help her carry home bagfuls of out-of-print books.

The elevator is unmanned from midnight until eight. Exiting into the austere main lobby, our shoes echo along the marble floor, but we don't wake the sole overnight doorman who's curled up asleep on a tiny cushioned bench with an unlit cigarette between two fingers.

It takes both Octavia and me to force the front door open. We squeeze through to the sidewalk. The day is gray, and streetlights illuminate a few cars and an M1 express bus soaring down Fifth Avenue. Walking south, I pull my mittens from my coat pockets. My sister pulls her scarf up to cover her cheeks. Her voice is muffled.

She says, "We really are going to The Cellar, but it's to find out how to fix you."

"Fix me?" I grab her around the shoulders. I can't hide my joy. "You mean you're not going to tell?"

Octavia flinches. Oops. Just because you admit why something scares you doesn't mean you stop being scared. I let her go.

"Sorry," I tell her.

"I'm sorry too. I don't want to feel the way that I feel. You don't want to be the way that you are. So, we'll fix you and get back to our normal lives."

I want a normal life. That's what Nick told me. He wants this phase to be over so he can start living for real. Yoon loves our life as it is. I've lived our life for one night, and I am not so sure that I want to be fixed. I kissed a boy. *The* boy. I had some nerve. But I can't lose my sister. But if I lose the cat inside me, will I go back to a safe, sedentary life filled with *could be*'s?

I say, "I don't think I can be fixed. Nick says I'll turn for five years, then stop on my own. Nick says I can suppress it with pot."

"*Nick says, Nick says.* How are you going to smoke pot? With what money? And where are you planning to light up? Not our room, Mary Jane. I'm not getting sent back to foster care because of drugs."

"We're not on parole. Mom and Dad aren't going to return us for smoking pot."

"No, they're going to send you back for being a mutant and me for being emotionally unstable. Remember when they got us, they said they'd take any healthy kid. Race and age didn't matter, but they knew their limitations. No autism, no handicaps. Where do you think your I'm-a-Teenage-Werewolf syndrome falls on that scale? If they catch you smoking, they'll want to know why. And you'll tell them. You can't keep a secret to save your life."

"What good has keeping secrets done you?" I shoot back—and instantly regret it.

Octavia frowns. Forty-five cats and lifelong scars. I feel terrible. That was a terrible thing to say.

"Why don't you let me try to find an answer for you first?" Octavia keeps the peace.

"Nick says—"

"*Nick says!*"

"Well, he does! Nobody else has told me what to do. He says Yoon's been researching since last summer but hasn't found much."

"Then, we'll go straight to the horse's ass and find out what Yoon knows. Believe me, he doesn't know everything. Nick either. There's a reason I'm the youngest-ever debate team captain at Purser-Lilley. I know where all the answers are buried."

chapter fourteen

The deli is full of club kids—not Lady Gaga groupies but boys getting home from playing cards in underground poker clubs. Poker clubs are regularly raided by cops and held up at gunpoint, but they reopen in new locations because boys will be boys. The players are primarily grown men, but sons of the Upper East Side with American Express black cards and bar mitzvah money to burn are always welcome. High school boys win big but lose big. Good or bad luck, they never tire. They sit at the tables, spit dip into sixteen-ounce Pepsi bottles, and play until dawn. Saturdays, they straggle home, trolling delis in search of sustenance. They are baggy-panted zombies.

Ben Strong is at the register with a Red Bull and a single-serving foil packet of Pop Tarts.

The deli owner says, "Brown sugar cinnamon, two-ninety-nine! Ask my son how he stays so skinny with this same breakfast every morning. He's out all night, like you! Needs sugar to keep going. Sleep keeps you going. But my son wants to find himself. Hah! I find him! Look! You find him too! There he is, filling flower buckets. His mother insists we sell flowers—two deliveries a week—so he can go to college!

You tell him if college isn't good enough for him, the navy is waiting! Next two years underwater!"

Octavia and I are at the entrance of the deli. Sure enough, to our right is Yoon with a garden hose. His thumb clogs the mouth of the hose. His hands are clad in his trademark yellow dishwashing gloves. He's in Nantucket Red khakis, rolled up to show his bare ankles in loafers. Waffle-textured long underwear sticks out of his lavender T-shirt, which must be part of a vintage collection. An iron-on wad of wasabi exclaims to an hourglass-shaped bottle: *You SOY crazy!*

I ask him, "Did Nick catch up with you?"

A grin flashes across Yoon's face. "I can't be caught."

His father shouts, "Overconfidence is deadly! You ask that mouse by the sour cream 'n onion how much longer he's going to be alive!"

Yoon drops the hose and darts past the ice cream freezer trunk, alongside the hot and cold salad bar, to the back of the deli. He crashes into the potato chip rack. Bags of Pirate's Booty plummet from the most expensive top shelf and land on and around Yoon, who lies on his belly, his chin to the floor, searching for the mouse underneath the cheap row of Wise.

The club kids crack up. Wired on caffeine, they down fistfuls of Cap'n Crunch straight from the box. Their Patagonia hiking jackets are covered with corn-colored crumbs. From their pockets, they pull rubber-banded rolls of $100 bills and IOU chits. They place bets on whether Yoon will catch the mouse, how quickly he'll do it, and whether he'll bring the mouse out from under the potato chip rack dead or alive.

Ben holds up a roll of bills as fat as a roll of Charmin. He says, "All of it if he eats it!"

The deli owner leans across the counter and snatches Ben's plastic bag of breakfast. He lords it over Ben's head. The deli owner is on a riser. Ben will have to reach up and hop to get his bag back.

The deli owner says, "You want him to eat a mouse, *you* catch it!"

Ben's friends roar. They wager Ben won't get within five feet of the potato chip rack. If he does, they wager he'll scream like a girl when he sees the little fella. If he faints, they wager on whether he'll fall headfirst into the banana bin or break his nose against the see-through fridge that holds the beer.

From the floor, Yoon says, "A week's salary says he catches it before me."

The club kids aren't impressed with what Yoon's put on the table, but they do the math. Minimum wage times five days a week plus overtime equals a rack of red $5 chips. Money is money, but easy money is the best. The club kids believe Yoon's made an impossible bet. He's bet on Ben to win. Even if Yoon throws the contest and doesn't catch the mouse, Ben must. Nobody believes Ben will shove his hand under the dark, low-lying, dust-bunny populated potato chip rack.

Except Yoon. He pats the rubber flood mat. There's plenty of room for two. He points under the rack. He says, "Come on, kid. Fish in a barrel."

Octavia says, "Don't do it, Ben. You might as well grab a sack of rabies."

Ben, who's been standing shell-shocked at the register with his penny change in his palm, is startled at my sister's voice. Apart from Ling Ling Lebowitz's verbal assaults and debate team sparing, girls don't strike up conversations with Ben.

"Don't let them pressure you," she adds.

"Tell you what, kid," calls Yoon. "You catch that mouse, and we'll split my winnings fifty-fifty!"

This doesn't ruffle the crowd. Even if the two of them cooked up a scam before everyone got here, it doesn't matter. Now that everyone *is* here and there is a mouse on the loose, the club kids know Ben is not going after it. The only time they've seen Ben be brave is at the poker table, when he bets pot into two aces on the flop. *Silly Yoon. Mice-catching is for killers.* The Ben we go to school with holds his pee all day if someone sees a water bug in the boys' restroom.

Octavia warns him: "Don't."

Ben chews the inside corner of his mouth. He's been waiting sixteen years for a chance to prove his manhood. He's certainly not going to prove it in gym, climbing the rope. He scans the deli impulse-buy rack for candy he could hurl at his prey with the accuracy of a tennis ball. He may want to slay a miniature dragon, but he doesn't want blood on his hands. He wants a story to tell at the poker table. He wants bragging rights. But most of all, he wants the club kids' money.

Me too.

Look at all those $100 bills held out in the air! All that cash would buy a huge bag of research from The Cellar or a huge bag of pot. Either way, I'd be afforded time off from the turning, which would keep my sister from turning on me.

I cry out, "I'll catch it!"

More of the club kids' money goes up. Expensive confetti. I hear it snatched and swapped. I see it—faded green. I smell it—sweet and warm, if warm is a smell.

Octavia grabs my elbow, but I jerk out of her grip.

Barreling through the club kids, I cry out, "Double or nothing!"

Ben says, "What about me?"

"You had your chance!"

I stop at Yoon's feet. He rolls onto his side, rests one hand on his hip, props his head in his other hand, and grins up at me.

Octavia shoots me her most incredulous, disgusted look. *Bitch, PLEASE!*

Ben steps away from the register. To save face, he should join Yoon and me at the back of the store.

Not on Octavia's watch. She can't stop me, but she'll stop him. She puts her hand on Ben's jacket sleeve. The club kids make whipping noises. Yoon meows like a—well, you know—but that meow is a little too spot-on, so he clucks like a chicken.

I say, "Move, Yoon."

The deli owner says, "Catching mice is not for girls."

Yoon says, "She's no normal girl, Father."

His velvet voice gets under my skin. It tingles up and down my spine. It makes me want to please him. I want to lie down beside Yoon and do what he says. My fingers rest on the corner of the hot and cold salad bar. Steam from the sautéed spinach and boiled half-ears of corn on the cob makes my hair frizz. Vinegar from the pickled cauliflower crinkles my nose.

Yoon says, "This girl is something special like me."

Club kids snicker. Compared to their rugby shirts and 501s, Yoon's clothes are flamboyant. The boys clearly aren't aware of what may or may not have gone on between Yoon and Mags behind this very potato chip rack. They certainly aren't aware of how good his tongue felt on my tail.

Yoon offers me his hand, and I extend mine. He slips off my mitten. I feel like he's untoggled my toggle coat and then fussed and fumbled with every button and zipper underneath. I wiggle my freed fingers. My hand itches to grab hold of the mouse. The want has nothing to do with money anymore. It's like I've discovered my hand was made only to open and trap. Yoon taps my index finger, and my hand heats with desire.

I drop to my knees, stretch out on my stomach. We are shoulder to shoulder. The flood mat presses zigzag patterns into our forearms and thighs. Ear to ear, we peer under the bottom rack.

The mouse is a baby, no bigger than a thimble and the same color as the floor.

Its tiny body palpitates with each desperate sniff. I've heard that mice are blind, that they sense their way by skimming walls with their whiskers. This little guy sees nothing. He's lost. He is dead center under the rack. For him, he has miles to run. The club kids' racket must be deafening. Mama! Where is his mama?

I don't care. That mouse smells like a nacho cheese–flavored Dorito.

"Take him, Kitty," Yoon whispers, his hot breath against my ear. "See how fast you are now."

His lips graze my earlobe. Then, his lips slip behind my ear, where the skin covers my skull. I feel a prick. My eyes tear, and I glance sideways at Yoon through the blur. He smiles and holds a thin, nearly invisible, stiff wire between his teeth. It is half the length of a toothpick. A whisker. It had sprouted out of the side of my head.

He whispers, "You're turning again."

Before my mind can process this, the mouse is caught in my hand.

I don't know how I got it. I wanted the mouse; the mouse is in my hand. The little critter squirms. Squeaks! His fur tickles my palm. His scrambling claws barely register on my skin. He noses his way through the hole that my curled fingers make. I seal the hole with my thumb the way Yoon plugged his garden hose.

Drawing my arm out from under the rack, Yoon helps me to my feet. He dusts me off. His hands swipe my coat sleeves, skirt hem, Mags's socks, and my naked knees. He doesn't pat my back. He slaps it. *Here, here! Get a load of yourself! Excitement's starting!* He grabs my wrist and raises it over my head. I pump my fist, my tiny trophy concealed inside.

The club kids go wild. Money funnels in my direction down the length of the salad bar. My sister turns away, repulsed. She wants to leave me.

The deli owner dumps Ben's breakfast out of the plastic bag and onto the counter. "Clean up on aisle one!" he shouts, flapping the bag.

Don't ask me why Ben takes the bag and walks toward me. Maybe because the deli owner is an adult, the boss, and Ben can't defy authority without a note from Ling Ling's doctor mom. Maybe getting the mouse from me is Ben's last shot at bravery. Standing in front of me, holding out the open bag, he expects me to fork over the mouse like a Hershey's Kiss on Halloween. No way. This is MY mouse. I tilt my head back, open my mouth, and toss the mouse up like a piece of popcorn.

A hand swipes the mouse from midair.

Yoon grabs me. His arms, long and sinewy, are different from Nick's. They are ropes, tight and strong. His ribs press through the back of my coat. I struggle to break free, but Yoon is an upright railroad track, and he has me tied. He forces me to see what I've lost. I am so mad, I could scream.

Octavia does that for me.

The mouse's tail twitches between Ben's closed lips. He hiccups, and the tail is gone. Before I can stop him, he swallows. He is showered with winnings that were rightfully mine.

chapter fifteen

The Webster Branch of the New York Public Library is a leftover, nineteenth-century mini-mansion. There are gas lamps to the right and left of the front door. The building is three stories, with giant vaulted windows revealing a children's reading room on the first floor. My sister goes to this library two or three times a week. I have not been inside a library in years.

I say, "I don't want to go in. I can smell the cellophane book wrappers from here."

"Get over it," Octavia snaps. "We're not going back to Yoon. *I told you* you're a hunter. I'm not letting him near you again. He'll bring out everything else that's bad about you. You're in my hands now."

She yanks open the front door, and I shuffle past her through the vestibule.

The circulation desk is manned by black and Hispanic teenage clerks. There are four of them scanning bar codes, unpacking transit holds, double-checking that the right number of CDs are with the proper audiobooks, and alphabetizing returns on the shelving cart. When they spot Octavia, they light up, wave, and mouth *Hey, girl!*

Octavia coos, "Haaaay!"

The clerks never stop working while Octavia loiters and chats with them about books, movies, TV—specifically *American Idol*. They all have different opinions on who's going to make it to Hollywood Week and who's going to crack under the pressure of group sing. The clerks don't ask to be introduced to me, and Octavia doesn't offer. These are her secret, outside-of-school friends, and she wants them to remain private.

Octavia asks, "Is Mrs. Wrinkles in The Cellar?"

"Always. But what do you want with her?"

Octavia motions to me.

"Oh, it's like that," one of the girl clerks says.

I'm not sure what she means, but apparently it is *like that* because Octavia doesn't say otherwise. My sister leads me down a wide marble staircase.

The Cellar Used Bookstore is one of New York City's best-kept secrets. Located in the Webster basement, all proceeds go to support local libraries. Along the far wall are hardbacks. To the left—jammed two rows deep, two on top of each other—are paperback mysteries. To the right are biographies, dramas, and histories. Rounding out the front: romance and sci-fi. Aisles are divided by chest-level antique bookcases filled with out-of-print classics. Nothing has a penciled price of more than two bucks. The bookstore is run exclusively by volunteers—retired, old-school, bespectacled librarians who no longer want to spend their days shushing the public. They play Broadway soundtracks and bustle about in matching work aprons that are printed with the silhouette of a cat whose tail drapes an open book like a bookmark.

"My dear!" a woman behind the sales counter exclaims. She beams at Octavia and clasps her hands together. She wears a cardigan over her work apron and has a handkerchief tucked up the cuff of her sleeve. Her hair is cropped short: a white, feathery swim cap. Large clip-on costume earrings dangle from her long lobes. Her glasses are tortoise shell and attached to a matching chain around her neck. Her face is a powder-dusted map of fine lines. Mrs. Wrinkles, I presume.

She pulls a stack of books out from underneath the counter. The books are tied with string, the way a box of cookies is tied at a bakery. She presents them to Octavia. "For the Dalton debate."

Octavia says, "You're the best."

"Say, *Thank you, Mrs. Wrinkles!*"

My sister repeats what the woman wants her to say softly—the softest I've ever heard Octavia speak. I can tell she's pleased with books—I've never heard of them and bet the Dalton debate team hasn't heard of them either—but Octavia's hesitant to take them. Her hand rests on the sales counter a few inches from the stack. The retired librarian nudges the stack toward Octavia's fingers, but Octavia jerks her hand away.

"My dear, how many times must we go through this charade? We both know you'll take what Mrs. Wrinkles has found for you. There's no reason to resist. There's no reason to feel frightened. There's nothing wrong with taking help. You asked and were answered. That's what The Cellar is for!"

I ask Octavia, "Does she do all your work for you?"

My sister scowls. "Yeah, she puts on blackface and does my trigonometry."

The older woman says to me, "You must need help if you're here with Octavia today. Tell me, my dear, what is it you need?"

I look to Octavia to speak for me. I can barely hear her when she says, "Mrs. Wrinkles."

"My dear, you need to *see* her?"

I'm confused. I thought we were talking to her.

Octavia says, "To be honest, I've never believed she was real."

"You and so many others, my dear. Yes, Mrs. Wrinkles is indeed very real. And now you want to meet with her—after all these years. Why now?"

"Something…weird…is happening to…someone I know." Octavia fiddles with the string on the bound lot of books. She's stumped over what to say next, how much more to say, or if she's already said too much.

The woman prompts her. "This something is happening to a friend?" She knows my sister's talking about me but, under anonymity, hopes Octavia will go on.

Octavia nods.

"This something scares you?"

Octavia nods.

"This something is something only Mrs. Wrinkles might understand?"

Octavia looks too frightened to even make a motion of *yes*.

"Oh, my dear, this must be serious."

"It is, Miss Ryan." My sister bites her lips and looks up at the ceiling in an effort not to cry.

Miss Ryan hurries out from behind the sales counter. She wraps her arms around my sister, who rests her head on Miss Ryan's shoulder, hides her face from me, and cries in earnest. Now *I'm* scared.

Miss Ryan asks, "Do you want me to come with you to see her, my dear?"

Octavia steels herself, draws her head back and shakes it *no*. She brings her coat sleeve to her nose, but Miss Ryan pulls her handkerchief from her sleeve, and Octavia blows her nose into that.

Miss Ryan says, "Chin up, soldier on." She gestures to a closed door at the rear of the room.

Octavia stares at the closed door but doesn't budge.

I take her hand and tug to get us going. If someone has answers about what's happening to me, scary or not, I need to find out.

Easing between antique bookcases, Octavia doesn't let go of my hand. Milk crates full of paperbacks line the aisle. We move slowly so as not to topple freestanding piles. I set my sights on a row of Stephen Kings against the far wall and give my sister's fingers a squeeze. She squeezes back. We're almost there. Whatever lies on the other side of that closed door frightens her more than me.

Opening the door, we find a smaller, narrower room of books. A smaller, narrower retired librarian sits at a smaller, narrower desk. *Whatever Happened to Baby Jane?* rouge is applied in smudgy circles upon her cavernous cheeks.

"Mrs. Wrinkles?" I ask.

The retired librarian raises her painted eyebrows. She squints over her Trident gum–sized, rimless eyeglasses, propped on the tip of her nose. She lets her gaze linger on Octavia, who is a quivering mess.

Octavia curtsies. So, I curtsy too.

The woman removes her hand from the huge book she is reading. All the books in here are thicker than thick and look to be written in Old English. This is where such books come to die. The old woman keeps her grip on an index card she's been using to read line by line. When she lifts her arm, a name tag emerges from behind her wide work apron strap. Miss Gibbs points us toward a doorway without a door that is blocked almost entirely by a bookcase.

This new chamber is equal to the size of my parents' bathroom but incredibly tall. Looking up at the skylight, I am at the bottom of a well. Perhaps this was once a terrarium. The room is tall enough to have housed a redwood. The shaft is bathed in daylight, but there is no artificial lighting. The shelves rise all the way to the top, but there is no ladder. All the books are coverless. A crumb of mortar falls along the wall. I peer into a sliver to find that the bookshelves give the illusion that the room is square, but it's circular.

"Young lady, may I help you?"

Octavia and I whip around to discover yet another retired librarian sitting on a swivel stool: an old man. We'd scooted right past him. He is inside this tower with us. He is no wider than the stool, and his three-piece, pinstriped suit makes him appear more elongated. His Windsor knot is as wide as his neck. No glasses. His eyes are thoughtful and rheumy. He clasps his hands over his crossed legs and bounces his top foot in want of an answer. He closes his eyes to better hear us, his dears. He smiles expectantly. Every line on his face grins.

I dare to ask, "Are you Mrs. Wrinkles?"

Octavia elbows me.

He chuckles. "Young lady, you *do* need help! I am Mr. Charles. *This* is Mrs. Wrinkles."

Placing his hand on his lapel, he opens his jacket a few inches from his chest. Out peeks the hairless head and shoulders of a sphynx.

Mrs. Wrinkles is not completely hairless. She is fuzzy like a peach. You can't see the fuzz, but you could feel it if you touched her—and she wants you to. As soon as she spots us, she slinks out of Mr. Charles's suit jacket, prances up his crossed leg, and preens on his knee like a Swiss goat on an Alp. She lifts her head. Her face is all angles. Her ears are tall and pointy, like the tips of a tiara. She can't weigh more than six pounds. Her skin is the palest of pinks, with faded black spots. She looks like a washed out, sun-bleached box of Good & Plenty. She extends a bony paw.

"Pleased to meet you," says Mr. Charles.

Octavia cowers behind me. I can see why Mrs. Wrinkles would scare her. The cat is straight out of King Tut's tomb. But she's so friendly! She paws the air and tilts her head inquisitively.

Mr. Charles says, "What, no fine-how-do-you-do's?"

Not shaking the cat's hand may be construed as rude on my part, but I am not doing it. I remember what happened to my shin when Yoon first visited me as the deli cat and then what happened to my legs when Peanut Butter and Jelly had a go. This morning, a stray whisker sprouted out of the side of my head. The turning has started. How many more hours do I have as myself? My body is ripening. If I touch Mrs. Wrinkles, my fingertips will look like I just ate a bag of Flamin' Hot Crunchy Cheetos.

I say, "I'm allergic. My sister's cat-phobic."

Mr. Charles says, "But Mrs. Wrinkles is no cat. She's a lady."

I hear Yoon's voice: *She's no normal girl, Father.*

I ask, "Is she human?"

Octavia punches me in the back.

"Is she what?" Mr. Charles chuckles. He rubs a faded black

spot between Mrs. Wrinkles's eyes. The sphynx purrs. With no fur, her ribs vibrate like a xylophone. He says, "Well, she's as smart as any human I've met. She knows exactly what I'm saying, don't you, Mrs. Wrinkles? And beautiful to boot!"

Mrs. Wrinkles lifts her narrow haunches to show off. She looks me up and down and sniffs. She must sense my inner cat like Peanut Butter and Jelly did, but she is indeed being a lady about it. No crying, no swarming, no pouncing, no hissing fits. The tip of her skinny tail runs up the center of her handler's face, but his eyes don't cross. He gingerly places his hands on her hips and rubs her like he's shining a shoe.

He says, "Mrs. Wrinkles has lived in this library all her life. She's sixteen years old. Her great-great—you can't imagine how many greats!—grandmother was kept by Miss Miriam Webster. Mimi purebred exotics. When she died, she donated her entire estate to the city on the condition that her darlings—and their darlings—be allowed to continue to live here. Mrs. Wrinkles is the last of her line."

Octavia peers out from behind me. "We need to ask her a question."

Mr. Charles says, "Be my guest."

"In private," she pleads.

"You have all the privacy you need."

"But you're here."

"I am her chaperone."

"You'll see what she gives us."

"Young lady, I have not seen anything since Jackie Kennedy was in the White House."

Mrs. Wrinkles flicks her tail back and forth, back and forth, like a hypnotist's pocket watch before Mr. Charles's eyes. His eyes don't move. This man is blind.

He says, "Even if I could see, I wouldn't say a word. Librarians never judge. We've sworn the same oaths as priests and doctors, but we keep our promises. Whatever is discovered here will remain confidential."

I lean forward and whisper to the sphynx, "Tell me about the turning."

Mrs. Wrinkles leaps onto a shelf packed with coverless books, their spines aligned according to height. There's an inch of space on the ledge, and she nails it. She doesn't wobble. Her balance is effortless. She leaps to a higher shelf on the case to the right, where larger books are crammed willy-nilly. She doesn't rustle pages hanging loose from poorly glued spines of what I'm guessing are atlases and maps of our bodies, ourselves. She springs to a higher shelf on the case to the right, this time landing on a book jutting out. The shelves get messier the higher she goes. More bird than cat, Mrs. Wrinkles flies from shelf to shelf, spiraling up and up and up.

Mr. Charles says, "My lady knows every inch of her house, knows where to find anything inquiring minds want to know."

The sphynx looks down and meows. The sound echoes

down the shaft. She's so high that her head is a postage stamp. Octavia gazes up and shades her eyes as if this will help her focus.

Mrs. Wrinkles ducks out of sight. I hear her claws sink into books as she climbs up the crawl space between the case and curved wall. Silence. She's stopped. Specks of dust glisten in the sunlight as they drift down three stories. A book nudges toward a shelf lip as Mrs. Wrinkles head-butts and paws at it from behind.

Octavia marvels, "I've always wondered, if she really *was* real, how she does it. You leave a question for her—"

"—and when the library closes," Mr. Charles finishes her thought, "Mrs. Wrinkles goes to work. This morning, we found your debate books laid out on the floor in the main Cellar room. My lady can ferret out anything, anywhere, no matter how small or how hidden."

Octavia says, "She's a hunter."

"For knowledge," says Mr. Charles.

Octavia nods, and although Mr. Charles can't see her, I think he senses a puncture in the air. I feel it. Since we got here, Octavia's fear has clogged this well like a fog. We all breathe easier because Octavia is slightly less afraid. She sees a bit of herself in Mrs. Wrinkles: a smart girl who finds comfort in the truth.

Books next to the one the sphynx has chosen for us jostle and threaten to fall. I duck and cover. Octavia presses her back against the shelves. Mr. Charles doesn't uncross his legs. His front foot keeps on bob-bob-bobbing along. Mrs. Wrinkles's book flaps as it falls three stories all by its lonesome. Mr. Charles sticks out his hand, as long and narrow as his shoe, and catches it.

It's a miniature—the size of one of those moving-image cartoon books you flip through to watch a stick figure slip on a banana peel. Mr. Charles holds it out to us between his index and writing fingers.

Octavia accepts it, opens it, and we peer inside.

In addition to the book's cover being torn off, the title page and table of contents have been ripped out. My sister turns the book over. The index is intact, but the words are made up of horseshoes, triangles, and pitchforks.

"It's in Greek," says Octavia.

She snaps the book shut.

The shadow of another cat's head drifts over the skylight like a storm cloud. The shadow is gigantic, imposing. One ear is missing a chunk. When the head turns to profile, a gaping mouth shows off shadowy canines as long as my arms. The room grows cold. We are eclipsed. Fear drapes my sister's face like a funeral veil.

Mr. Charles says, "Damn that tomcat always coming around! He thinks our lady is getting old. He wants us to adopt him as soon as she passes on to that great litter box in the sky. But we hate that tomcat, and our lady isn't going anywhere anytime soon, are you, Mrs. Wrinkles?"

Mrs. Wrinkles rolls onto her back and braces her paws on the shelf above. She shimmies out so her hips balance on the flatness of a book. Her stomach muscles support her top half in midair. Her ribs rumble like a purr, but a purr it is not. She thrashes the air beneath the Great-and-Powerful-Oz–sized shadowy head. Her anti-purr sours into a challenge.

Mrowl! Break the skylight. Mrowl! Spatter me with broken glass. Mrowl! Jump! Come and get me. I dare you! Mrowl! I wish you would!

The tomcat bellows. I don't get meaning from him. I get sheer meanness. He sounds like a dragon. I expect to get cooked. At any second, the skylight glass will melt, pour down the well, and solder me to the floor.

Not Octavia. She's squeezed out of the well. Books topple from the Old English graveyard bookcase that blocks the doorframe. I hear her apologize to Miss Gibbs and then she is gone.

I have to go after her. She has the Greek book.

chapter sixteen

Outside, braced against the handicap ramp railing, Ben's got Octavia.

Wait, *what?* Yes, here he is with crazy, coincidental timing straight out of the movies.

Octavia had been running and, I guess, ran right into him. He'd caught her. They both look surprised. There is distance between their bodies, but his hands are secured to her shoulders. Octavia doesn't pull away. She clutches the lapels of his camel-hair coat, which he now wears instead of his poker parka. They aren't looking at each other. They aren't looking at me either. In light of what's looming above, I guess Octavia's forgiven or momentarily forgotten Ben's eating a mouse.

From the library roof, a mammoth tomcat hangs, gargoyle-style, over the edge.

The tomcat is bigger than Yoon when he turns. He sets to stalking the ledge to show off his length and muscles. He cracks his tail like a whip. His yellow eyes narrow. His face is flattened as if he's taken more than his share of punches. His right ear is half-eaten by mites, but he's healthy now. His fur is glossy and undefiled. He is entirely one color.

"Meet Country Club," says Nick.

"Wait, *what?*" I actually say it aloud this time. Again, a boy has seemingly stepped out of nowhere. *The* boy. MY boy. I ask him, "What are you doing here? Are you with Ben?"

Nick says, "I owe him."

"Poker?"

Nick cocks his head at me. He hasn't washed his hair since last night. His curls are stiffer and stand on end. He gently takes hold of my wrist as if he does it all the time. He twirls me into his chest so that my back aligns with his front. *Silly Mary.* How can I talk about something as trivial as poker at a time like this?

We look up at the tomcat, who glowers down at us. Nick rests his chin on my shoulder. His warmth radiates up my neck and pinches my earlobe. The sensation is familiar and heady. Momentarily, I don't care about the tomcat like I didn't care about Ling Ling when Nick held me this exact same way on the terrace last night. I could turn my head and kiss him—but I want to know what's going on.

I ask, "Why *Country Club?*"

"Earth to Rosa Parks," says Octavia. "That cat is white-only!"

Country Club bellows. There is no *mmm* in his mrowl. His mouth opens, and a dark noise issues forth—a menacing, guttural, unending roar. His canines are swords. If he bit you, those teeth would hit bone. He'd take out your ankle with one lock of his jaw. He is prehistoric.

Strangers stop in the cold to look up at the beast. Country Club is the closest thing to Godzilla these real-life Upper Eastsiders have seen. Babies are clutched and wheels of $1,600 strollers put to the test. Coffee sip-tops pop off and scald trembling hands. People trip and curse the sidewalk. Earpieces are pressed, calls made to 911 for the fire department and 311 for animal control. Some dumbass throws a rock.

The tomcat takes no notice.

Nick clasps his hands around my stomach and hugs me. He burrows his face into the side of my neck. His curls tickle. This may read as a protective gesture—impassioned, even— but that is not how it feels. I am not being snuggled. I am being restrained.

Oh.

I get why.

I am tingling.

From neck to knees.

With rage.

I want to bait and switch Country Club within an inch of his life. How dare he threaten Mrs. Wrinkles? Who is he to bellow at me? This is MY library! MY neighborhood! MY sister! MY…boyfriend? Is that what Nick is? And what exactly is Ben to me? Never mind now. It doesn't matter. Country Club is nothing but a bunny. I want all four of his feet on a key chain.

I wriggle and buck.

Nick secures me in place. His breath on my neck is as hot as a hair dryer.

I hop, raise my knees, kick back, and jam my heels into his shins. Nick exhales sharply but doesn't let go.

Strangers filter off the library sidewalk, covering their mouths as they report our obnoxious behavior into their cells. New Yorkers will stick around for a gargantuan cat, but they're not getting sucked into a couple of dumb kids horsing around. They think we're asking for it. That tomcat's going to jump and then we're really going to be sorry. I laugh at their stupidity. I jerk and writhe and strain to break free from Nick's tight hold. I'm going to tear that tomcat apart!

"Are you crazy?" exclaims Octavia from her resting spot on Ben's coat lapel.

"I don't know," I admit.

Country Club sits stoically and studies me. His eyes are yellow slits, his breathing controlled. If you didn't know he was there, you might not even notice him. If you did, you'd mistake him for a fake owl that people put on their fire escapes and roofs to scare away rats. He antagonizes me with his composure.

I kick Nick again.

"Damn it, Mary! Quit!" Nick grips me with such force that he bends backward over the handicap railing and pulls me along with him. The toe bumpers of his red Chuck Taylors steady us on the cement ramp, but my feet are in the air. I bicycle my legs! I kick, kick, and kick! I scream to be released. Nick whispers, "It's the orange."

I feel it, tingling, sprouting, bristling: a stripe from my shirt tag up the back of my neck.

He whispers, "You can't help it, but you have to. Orange means you could take him, but you're too little now. If you touch him, you'll turn. He'll *kill you* if you turn."

"Just let me go!"

Octavia takes her hands off Ben and grabs at my flailing ankles. Ben sticks his hands between me and her to try to protect Octavia from getting booted in the face. She gets hold of a calf, drops to the ground, and drags me with her. My butt hits cement. For crying out loud, how quick was I to forget that I'm still in my wrinkly, stinky, school skirt from yesterday? Through the children's reading room windows, slack-jawed first graders are still gaping from getting a gander at my drawers.

Sirens blare in the distance.

Well, what do you know? Even in Manhattan, a wild cat gets a one-alarm fire department response. Animal control wheels up behind the laddered truck. Tranquilizer guns are drawn. A fireman cranks the big bolt on a hydrant. The long, flat hose is unwound and aimed. Two firemen storm into the library. Weighed down by fifty pounds of gear, their footfalls land heavily on the stairs as they pound their way up through adult fiction and nonfiction to get to the roof.

Country Club doesn't look nervous. *Perturbed* is more like it.

I've seen that expression before on Yoon's deli cat face. On Yoon, it was appropriate. He'd escaped falling into my toilet and then the plastic slats on the twins' terrace lounge chair. Country Club has a hard rush of water, semi-poisonous darts, and ax-yielding firemen coming his way. But he glances back at me as if these are minor distractions at best.

"Let her rip!" shouts a fireman. The hose fattens with water.

The animal control people aim their tranquilizers and pull their triggers. They look even more frightened than the pedestrians. Feathered needles arch toward the roof. Every shot misses.

Country Club pays the ammunition as much mind as he paid the dumbass's rock. He turns and holds his tail high so we can all see his insubordinate butt.

But I notice that something is missing. Two things are missing really. What's round and white and fuzzy all over? Nothing on this cat. If there was ever a doubt in my head that Country Club is more than a cat—something like Nick, Yoon, and I are—that doubt is snip-snipped.

Country Club flicks his tail as the stream from the firemen's hose, raised toward the roof, splatters the building. When the stream hits the ledge, it explodes and makes a rainbow. Country Club is misted but saunters out of sight before he gets a full blast. The roof door bangs open. There's shouting, but the arriving firemen are too slow to catch him as he springs to freedom on neighboring roofs.

chapter seventeen

Nick skims the tiny Greek book Octavia took from the library. He says, "I can't read this. It's in ancient Greek."

Ben asks, "What are you looking for exactly?"

"It doesn't matter. If Mary wants help and I can help her, I will. We'll go to my house and have Papou translate."

I say, "Your grandmother's not going to be happy to see me."

Nick says, "Why, because you got me in trouble at school? Once she finds out how much we're alike, she'll forget all about the principal's office."

I self-consciously touch the orange fuzz on the nape of my neck.

To help hide the skinny stripe behind my long hair, Nick offers me his scarf; the same black-and-gray-checked scarf he wouldn't let Ling Ling borrow on the bus outside my house. No matter how hard she tugged at it, he wouldn't give it to her. Now it's tied around my neck. Instantly, it itches. But I'll put up with the irritation. This scarf is Nick's way of showing the world he belongs with me.

"It's cheap," Nick confirms, "but Yiayia's so proud of herself for getting a deal." He impersonates her. "*Ela! TWO for ten dollars, I talked the salesman into!*"

Octavia says, "Let's go already."

I say, "I don't want Ben to hear what the book says."

Ben says, "Sorry, Mary, you're not getting rid of me. Nick told you he owes me."

Octavia hails a cab. "We're wasting time. Everybody get in already! You'll get yours, Ben, and we'll get ours."

Nick gives his address to the taxi driver, dives into the back seat, and scoots to the far door. He pats the hump. What else can I do but pile in after him? Octavia crams in after me. She's none too happy to be holed up with two cat people. I know she blames Nick for what's happening to me and for what will happen to her if we don't get me fixed. She yanks the door closed, leans forward, and glares around me at him.

Ben, who's left to sit in the front, sinks into the passenger seat and frowns into the rearview mirror. Racing uptown, the bulletproof partition, taxi radio, and driver's never-ending, one-sided conversation into his earpiece will make it impossible for Ben to hear us.

I ask Nick, "Who's Country Club's chaperone?"

"He doesn't have one. He's stray."

"If he's stray, what about his…who cut off his…"

"Nuts," Octavia says in a way that makes Nick cross his legs.

"I don't know," he says. "He either spent time in a pound or someone neutered him as a kitten and then left him to fend for himself. He lives down on Ludlow. But since the economy tanked, he's been up here sniffing around."

"For what?"

"New territory. Haven't you noticed? The Upper East Side is mostly vacant lots. There are empty stores on every block. The worst stretch is on Lex between 72nd and 77th. Every other window in your neighborhood is dark. Caviarteria, Starwich—"

"That bathing suit store," I think out loud. "The antique jewelry store…that store with retro furniture."

"Payard," murmurs Octavia. "Every damn day, I miss those chocolate croissants."

Nick says, "No more mom-and-pops. Papou says we're the new Lower East Side minus the bad element. But the bad element's already here. Country Club is King of the Strays."

"You mean *them*?"

"Yeah."

"So, who are *we*?"

"If you're with me—"

"I'm with you!" The words fly out of my mouth. "I mean, why wouldn't I be with you?"

"If you're with me, you're a *dom*. As in *domestic*," Nick explains.

"Domestic," Octavia repeats, "because you guys live at home?"

"Yeah. We're fed, taken care of, given a roof over our heads. Spoiled, in strays' opinions." He studies the time, temperature, and fare on the front seat's flat screen TV and decides what to reveal next. "See, doms and strays—the sides, us and them—

are made up of *pure-cats*, like Country Club, and *turn-cats*, like you and me."

"Turn-cats, that's what we're called?"

Octavia mutters, "Y'all need help."

Nick twists in his seat and snaps: "That's right. We do need help, but we don't have any! Apart from your little library book, there's no written history about what we are. We're not werewolves."

Octavia swallows hard. "Are there werewolves?"

"Hell if I know."

I ask, "So, the twins' cats are domestics?"

Nick nods. "Peanut Butter and Jelly."

"You know them?" says Octavia.

"Those Kim Jong-Il–lookin' crybabies? Yeah."

"And Mrs. Wrinkles?" she breathes.

"Queen of the Doms. Her family's ruled for thirty years; Country Club has ruled the strays for a week. He's only four years old, but talk about your dictators. His cats won't lick themselves without his permission."

My heart starts to thump. "Who are the stray turn-cats?"

Nick leans back. "Runaways. Kids who waste their lives on the benches outside American Apparel down on Orchard. You know the type: faces pierced, tattooed, dreaded-up, dirty. They left home for some kind of freedom, but I don't know what kind of freedom you get by sleeping in abandoned buildings. This isn't the eighties.

They're not starving artists. When their turn-time is up, where will they be?"

Uh-oh. A chink in Nick's shining armor. If it weren't for my parents, where would I be? I am a lottery kid. My parents plucked me like a numbered ping-pong ball out of hundreds of thousands of foster kids, who are now living who knows where under who knows what kinds of conditions. No one chooses to run away. You run because you have no choice; continue living where you are living is worse than living on the streets. It is hell. But the streets are worse than hell. To avoid them, Octavia spent a year with the devil's minions.

She says, "Maybe those turn-kids were kicked out when their folks found out what they were."

Nick says, "Maybe. But that's not our problem. Our problem is them turning up here. They need to stay below Houston where they belong. But Country Club wants his strays to squat in our empty lots."

I remember what Mr. Charles said about Country Club. "He wants to take over. He thinks Mrs. Wrinkles is getting old."

"She is. Best-case scenario, in a few years, she'll die of natural causes. After her, there are no more Webster Wrinkles. A new dom has to take her place."

"Has a turn-cat ever ruled?"

"Not the doms. With strays, power goes back and forth between pures and turns all the time. Strays love to fight. A turn-cat had power before Country Club killed him. He murdered that kid in cold blood when he was human. It was gruesome."

My body tenses. "You saw?"

"Yoon dragged me downtown to the stray royal lair to see an initiation."

Stray royal lair? I can only imagine what Octavia is thinking. I keep my attention focused on Nick. We're close to his house. Five more blocks.

"Why'd you go with him to begin with?" I ask.

"I don't know many turns. Before you, I was the only one at Purser-Lilley. Yoon pisses me off, but he understands me. Sometimes, I need that companionship. I try to stay out of the whole doms-versus-strays situation, but Yoon is hard to say no to."

"But he's one of them."

"Officially, he's *on the fence.* He runs with strays but lives at home. He does enough to keep the strays happy, so they let him stick around. To officially become a stray if you're a turn, you have to be *marred.* Yoon wanted me to see that initiation ceremony because he thought it would impress me."

"Did it?

"It did. I'll never go back to Kropps & Bobbers again."

"Where?" Octavia grumbles.

"Hair salon down on Ludlow. There's an overgrown garden in the back with high walls where stray turns and pures hang out. The owner is an animal lover; a people lover too. She doesn't judge. She keeps the back door closed, looks the other way, and doesn't ask questions."

"So, what happened?" Octavia now wants to know, twisting toward him.

Nick's eyes get so sad, it's got to be impossible for Octavia not to pick up on how much he hates how we are and how hopeless he thinks our situation is. But if it weren't for our condition, Nick would never have sought me out. We would never have kissed. I wouldn't be tingling—in the good way—from being pressed up beside him. I wonder if the Greek book has a cure, and if he and I get fixed, will we stay together. Or will he ignore me? Because every time he sees me, he'll remember what he wants to forget.

Nick explains, "To get initiated into the strays, you have to mar yourself with a characteristic of the current king or queen. So, if the king's a bobcat, you have your tail cut off. If the king's a Persian, you have your nose broken. You know how Hussein had all those look-alikes? Strays call it getting *Saddam-ed.*"

Octavia says, "That's disgusting! Why would Yoon want to be one of them?"

"Because strays are wild and unaccountable to anyone but each other. Apart from turning, once you're a cat—I'll admit it—it feels good. Everything feels better."

"Like love?" I dare to ask.

Nick looks at me with his sad eyes. He says, "When you're a cat, there is no love. Just lust. Heightened senses and no morals.

You live life in *the now*. Strays want to live that way forever, but most of them don't make it through their turn-time alive. The last king was a rotten little shit. Fifteen but built like he was nine. He fought everyone. His front two teeth were knocked out, so he spat when he spoke. Country Club was his biggest protector. The kid had nursed his mite-infested ear back to health to gain his loyalty, but this one time, he left Country Club out in the snow. To a cat, rain feels like razor blades, but snow feels even worse. Country Club nearly died. And cats aren't dogs. They're spiteful. They never forgive.

"So, Yoon and I are downtown in that salon's back garden, crowded around the initiation ceremony with a bunch of strays—turns in human form and pures in their only form—and we're all watching the king stick a pair of pliers in some idiot's mouth. That's when Country Club jumped him. Landed square on the king's head. His weight broke his neck, but before the king hit the ground, Country Club had scalped him, skinned his face, and nearly torn his head clean off."

Octavia warns, "Mary, you cannot be part of this."

Bile rises in my throat, the soured acid of my last meal—ham and cheese Hot Pockets. My desire to fight Country Club is nothing more than a bad taste in my mouth. If Nick hadn't held me back from running after him at the library, what would that huge white monster have done to me? What made me think I could take him? What made me want to fight him at all?

The orange, Nick had whispered.

I slip off a mitten and reach back to touch the fuzz on the nape of my neck. The orange stripe has crept up behind my ears into the shape of a slingshot.

Nick lifts my hair, peels down the scarf, and takes a look. The gesture is incredibly intimate. Heat spills down my throat and under my blouse.

He says, "It's spreading."

Octavia shouts, "Get your hands off her!"

Nick pulls away. "It's not me who started it! She can't catch it from me when I'm like this."

Like this. I glance beside me and take him in. Nick Martin. Nick Martin. Nick Martin! Medium-height, medium-dark, and pretty-gosh-dang-close-to-handsome. I twist my head toward Octavia. All she sees is filth dressed up like a boy doll.

She says, "Mary, we have to fix you. We have to fix you right now."

Her hand opens and closes around the door handle. She's debating whether to jump out at the next red light and pull me along with her. Her other hand grips the tiny Greek book in her lap. Apart from Papou, we don't have any other translators at the ready. If I'm going to be fixed, he's the one to tell me how. Octavia knows I'm turning. She doesn't want to see my full transformation again.

Nick reaches across me and grabs Octavia's hand with the tiny book. "Only physical contact with cats can start Mary off."

"Get off me!" Octavia shrieks, jerking away.

"It doesn't matter if I touch you—nothing will ever happen."

"But I didn't touch Country Club," I point out.

"But you wanted to. Urges to be a cat will make you turn too."

I think about the whisker Yoon plucked from my head. His nearness didn't put it there; it was my urge to catch the mouse. The fur on my neck grew from my thirst for Country Club's blood. The turning is upon me. And now it's spreading on its own.

Nick says, "You're a kitten. Each time you turn, the turning will come quicker. Your cat self will get bigger. The more full-grown cat you become, the easier the turning will be to control. Eventually, in season, you'll be able to turn without triggers whenever you want."

Octavia asks, "How long has she got before she turns this time?"

"If she doesn't touch a cat or get herself in a situation where she wants to be a cat, she should have until tonight."

"But if she does?" Octavia pleads.

"It depends." Nick's voice is even, without emotion. It's such self-control that keeps his own fear at bay. "On the circumstances, her level of exposure, how bad she wants it. Could be hours, could be minutes."

"No," Octavia decides. "It is not going to happen, Nick. Your grandfather's going to read the Greek book and tell us how to stop it."

Nick says, "I hope you're right."

chapter eighteen

Nick's yiayia opens the front door to their townhouse. Out from under her mink, the old woman appears more formidable. She wears thick-heeled, lace-up ankle boots. Her calves are covered by knee-highs a few shades darker than her natural skin color. Her housedress looks like something Mom would describe one of her characters wearing when she's bludgeoned to death by a neighbor who's sick and tired of lending her cups of sugar.

Yiayia waves us in out of the cold toward the mudroom. As I suspected, she is not happy to see me. She eyes the warped hem of my plaid skirt and my wrinkled cardigan when I take off my coat. In Manhattan, you'll see a murderous tomcat on the roof of a library before you see a girl in her school uniform on the weekend—much less one as messy as mine. Who knows where she thinks I spent last night and why she's imagining I haven't been home to change. My skirt stinks from being crumpled on the twins' terrace, laid out on the deli floor, and doused by dust in The Cellar book well.

Yiayia crinkles her nose and says, *"Poofu, poofu."*

Nick says, "Yiayia, be nice. You remember Mary. This is her sister, Octavia. You know Ben from gymnastics."

"Benjamin!" She ignores the Richards sisters. "Mr. Rope Climber Who Couldn't! Legs better?" She pinches his lean upper arm. "Let Yiayia feed you! In the oven, I have pastitsio: Greek lasagna, but instead of tomato sauce, it's béchamel. Five pounds you'll leave with!"

The mudroom is stuffed. Every hook and cubbyhole is taken. Umbrellas lay open like super-sized shiitake mushrooms turned upside down. Black, navy, and brown winter coats line the walls. Crammed in between is a shiny pearl version of the Michelin Man down jacket, with a rabbit-fur lined hood, owned by Nick's mother. On the bench sits her blood-red, five-grand lambskin designer status symbol. I imagine Nick's mom sporting it with stiletto boots and skinny jeans; bending over, her hot pink, Hanky Panky whale tail embarrassing her son.

Yiayia notices Nick's scarf still tied around my neck. She touches the fringe and pulls her fingers away like the strands are barbed wire. She says, "Nico mou, what are you doing? What are you thinking?"

Nick doesn't answer her.

To me, she says, "My Nick is to catch pneumonia because you don't want to look like you care that it's cold?"

I don't say anything.

"Ela. Hand it here."

I don't take off the scarf.

"Ela!"

She may know Nick's secret, but she doesn't know mine. Ben for sure doesn't know. If he sees the orange fur on the back of my neck, the rest of my life will be reduced to a series of prop bets for him and the club kids.

Nick says, "Yiayia, it's fine."

"Oh, fine is what it is? It is fine for you to toy with a young girl's heart?"

Wait. Who's she mad at? Me or him?

She says, "Take your girl upstairs to Papou and see how fine you think it is. See what he has waiting for you. A maybe or maybe not so nice surprise. Go on, all of you."

Nick says, "Ben's going to wait with you in the kitchen."

"*Oxi!* Nothing doing. You brought him into this house, he stays with you. He is your guest. You treat him that way. Your mother doesn't mind your manners, but I do!" She gestures to the stairs. "Ela! All of you! Climb! Papou is at the top."

Ben asks, "Five flights?"

Yiayia crosses her arms and appraises him. "Do not be the weakling others say that you are."

The Martins' stairwell is a hodgepodge: a junk drawer of everything they own with a hook that they don't want to display in the main rooms—family photo collages, silver- and gold-cast icons of Mary and the baby Jesus, and small oil paintings of the Acropolis, fishing boats, and old women in black kerchiefs on stoops.

Ben breathes heavily as we reach the fifth floor. Static-filled opera music drifts out of the study. It's the WQXR live matinee broadcast from the Met. Inside, Papou is stretched out on an Eames chair and ottoman and waves his weatherworn hands, conducting the music. He ignores the four of us as if we are latecomers. Intently, he keeps his eyes on the show.

I am sickened by what he sees.

Before him, true diva that she is, Ling Ling Lebowitz lip syncs "Poor Little Buttercup" from *HMS Pinafore*. Her dark purple bra cups show through her tank top. Wrapped around her throat is Nick's other black-and-gray-checked scarf.

"Aw, hell no!" says Octavia.

I want to run. I have to get out of here. Nick's scarf is too tight around my own throat. It itches. It's strangling me! I want to rip it off and throw it out the window. I want to jump out after it. I don't care if I break my legs. I don't care if I never speak to Nick again. I don't care if I never get a translation from Papou. I'd rather be a freak of nature for the rest of my life than spend one more minute in this room with Ling Ling and her identical two-for-one scarf.

When did Nick give it to her? Before he came to see me on the twins' terrace? When he wouldn't say her name? When he said he didn't care what she liked? When I asked him if they were together and in answer he held my hand? How could he? Mislead me? Lie to me? Kiss me? How could he give me a scarf when he gave her one too?

Nick asks her, "What are you doing here?"

Ling Ling asks, "What are they doing here? You're my boyfriend."

"I'm not your boyfriend."

"Until you give me what I want, you are what I say you are," she says, marching over to the stereo and shutting it off.

Papou says, "Children, be civil. You are not animals."

"At least, not right now," Ling Ling mutters.

Nick glares at her. She's hit a nerve—for me too. Does she share our bond too? Is she wearing his scarf to cover up proof that she's turning like me? I have to find out! I have to see her hidden skin! I lunge at her.

I don't know how I get hold of her scarf. I wanted the scarf; the scarf is in my hand.

It tightens like a noose around Ling Ling's neck.

She's so light, I jerk her to her tiptoes.

She pulls back.

I jerk her to me.

She clamps her hands on my forearms. She's no match for my strength, but her nails are filed to sharp points. She sinks them into my flesh. I grit my teeth. I won't let her drive a scream out of me. Nick grabs me from behind. Papou grabs Ling Ling. They try to pry us apart, but we won't be separated. I want her scarf off! I cling to it with both hands. She wants to make me scream. Nick and Papou persist at trying to break up our fight, but then Ling Ling drags her nails along my arms.

I cry out and let go of her.

Her body goes limp.

Papou unhands her.

She comes at me again.

She grabs MY scarf. It comes off my neck with her weight when she drops to the rug. I drop with her. She scrambles on top of me. She straddles me. Her fingernails fly. I shield my face. She bends forward, her face so close to mine, I smell gummy cherries on her hot, ragged breath. Her bleach-blond bangs blind me as she scours my skin. Ling Ling knows what I've been looking for on her because now she is looking for it on me.

I stop fighting. Let her find it.

She wraps her hands around my throat. When her fingers touch the fur on the nape of my neck, she tips off of me, lands on her side, and cries. Hysterically. She becomes a blubbering mess. I swear I think she'll drown in her tears. She chokes as she screams at Nick: "Whyyy?"

Nick reaches into the heap that is Ling Ling and me. I raise my injured arms. Rivulets of blood roll from my wrists toward my elbows and pool in the bunched cuffs of my school shirt and cardigan. I feel like I'm eight again and testing Dad's love. But Nick chooses Ling Ling. He hooks her hands around his neck, cushions her head against his chest, scoops her up, and carries her to the couch.

I want to disappear. I want to go home.

Octavia takes me by the elbows and helps me stand. She steers me to sit in the chair in front of Ben. Papou places the desk blotter across the arms of the chair. He rests my ruined arms on giant sheets of notepaper. Blood seeps from my wounds onto doodles of turtles and snails. Papou presses an intercom button that leads to the kitchen.

"Nai?" Yiayia's crackling voice blares.

Papou says what I assume are the Greek words for peroxide and bandages.

Nick sits beside Ling Ling and rocks her. She's still got his scarf around her neck. She covers her face with the fringe ends and sobs. Nick says, "Shh. Don't cry. I can't stand it when girls cry."

As soon as Ling Ling hears this, she completely loses her shit.

Nicks looks to me. "She's just jealous."

Ling Ling cries, "I am not!"

Nick gets up, and Ling Ling falls onto the warm spot he left. She grabs his wrist and pulls, but he won't sit back down. She cries, "Okay, I am! I'm jealous! Is that what you want to hear? Is that what you all want to hear?" She begs Nick, "How did you do it? Tell me! You said you couldn't give it to me, but you gave it to her!"

"Mary had it before we got together."

"You *got together?*" Ling Ling's face slackens. Her contraband lipstick darkens as her skin drains of color. She's sickened by her visions of our kisses, searching hands, partial nakedness, and much, much more than what went on between us. She drops her head between her knees. She moans, "How could you?"

Nick says, "I didn't have any choice."

"There's always a choice."

Octavia says, "What makes you so sure?"

Ling Ling turns her anger on my sister. "Just who do you think you are all of a sudden? You don't belong here. There's nothing special about you. Your birth mom didn't want you enough to even give you a name. You were number eight, *Octo*-avia, so that's what she called you."

Octavia says, "Your birth mom was too stupid to remember your name, so she named you twice."

Papou says, "Please! Ladies, civility. You're not—"

"Animals? We know," says Ling Ling, "but the rest of them are."

"The rest of them?" says Octavia. She looks at me.

I look at Nick.

He looks at Ben. Ling Ling looks at the skinny, kid squirreled behind the chair too.

Ben shrugs. His hands disappear behind the suede backing. His belt buckle clanks as he unhooks the catch and pulls out the strap. His button fly pops open. He shifts his weight from foot to foot and slips off his jeans. When he steps out, his monogrammed Seize sur Vingt boxer shorts read *BS*. His rope burns have healed overnight. All that's left, from his thighs to his ankles, are faint lines highlighted by dense stripes of silvery blue cat fur.

chapter nineteen

B en's a Russian Blue," says Nick.

"Just the once," says Ben.

"Dude, check your legs. You're turning again."

"How?"

Nick raises his eyebrows. He looks from me to Ling Ling. My busted oxford shirt is open to reveal the front clasp of my bra. Ling Ling's tank top is drooped over one shoulder. We're disheveled. We've fought a girl fight. Ben can't help how his body has reacted. Although not specific to boy human or boy cat, he's had an urge.

Ling Ling says, "Perv."

Ben turns his back to us and hops into his jeans.

Octavia walks right over to Ling Ling and slugs her in the arm. I guess my sister's been shocked and scared by so many cats so many times today that she's not overwhelmed by Ben's *ta-da*. Or maybe, no matter what form he takes, he'll always look the same to her: a picked-on kid who could use some friendly support. Or maybe she's moved on from fear to unadulterated anger and decided to take it out on Ling Ling.

I wish I'd hit Ling Ling myself.

Ling Ling cries, clutching her arm. "It should be me, not Ben! Not Mary! It's meant to be me! I was adopted for a reason! It was fate I was at Kropps & Bobbers getting my hair dyed when I was! I saw what happened out back because it's supposed to happen to me!"

I say, "You saw a kid murdered."

"No," Ling Ling chokes out. "I saw Nick turn."

"*She* saw?" Now it's me who's close to crying. This is more than Nick sharing an identical scarf. This is him sharing what and who we are at our core. I yell at him, "You stole my breath so *I* wouldn't see!"

Nick says, "I didn't mean for it to happen. Country Club killed the king, and we all turned and ran. Turned, as in *turned*. Then, I had an asthma attack. I only have them when I'm a turn. When I get asthma, I can't move, Mary. My body seizes up. I'm stuck wheezing in place until the attack goes away. I looked up, and Ling Ling was standing in the back salon doorway, and I heard sirens coming. I was helpless! She picked me up and shoved me in that big-ass bag of hers. She took me home and made me tell her everything and give her the nip with the hope that it would trigger something inside her that isn't there. She's been threatening to expose me, to expose all of us, if I don't turn her too."

"Can you? Is there a way?"

"No. But Ling Ling won't believe me because Country Club's strays have been leading her on."

Ling Ling asks a very good question. "Why would they promise me the impossible?"

Nick looks at her coldly. "Why do you think?"

I flash back to Ling Ling being passed between Nick and three boys, apparently three stray turns, outside my parents' bathroom window. I wonder if Nick was with her to protect her or if she blackmailed him into coming along. I can see by her expression that she remembers doing more than spooning with those boys. The stray turns must have had an unending list of requests. Ling Ling must have made her own list for Nick. Slumped on the couch, she looks ashamed of herself. She readjusts her tank top to cover her bra strap. She removes Nick's scarf from her neck and modestly wraps it around her shoulders.

I ask Nick, "How could you not tell me about Ben?"

"Same reason I didn't tell him about you. It's his news to tell."

"Well, he obviously knew about me or he wouldn't have tagged along."

"Nick didn't tell me," Ben says, stepping out from behind the chair. "I figured it out at the deli. After you left, Yoon confirmed it. I guess he's not as discreet as Nick, but he is the one who helped me turn the first time."

"When?" asks Octavia.

"Last night, before poker. I stopped by the deli on the way to a club. This cat comes out from under the potato chip rack and starts circling my legs. He pushes his face up under my pants cuffs. Then, I start…"

"Tingling?" I suggest.

"Yeah! Then itching like crazy. The rope burns were like highways for the fur. It was like my legs were dipped in—"

"Fire ants?"

He laughs, overcome with relief that someone knows what he's been through. "I was going to say hornets, but fire ants are good. Next thing I know, I've blacked out. I come to in an alley. I thought I was hallucinating. Like maybe that Jamaican lunch lady finally flipped her lid and hoodooed the fruit punch. But then Yoon helped me turn back to my regular self. He explained a lot. Then, Nick showed up."

I ask Nick, "You said you picked up my scent at Purser-Lilley. You must have smelled Ben's. How could you let Yoon get to him first?"

Nick says, "Yoon got to *you* first. And as far as scents go, he'll always be able to track you. Like onions in a flower bed."

"Do I stink?" I ask, humiliated.

"No, Mary, you smell incredibly good. Your scent is stronger than any I've ever smelled. At school, I didn't know about Ben because your scent overpowers his."

"*Mazel tov,*" says Ben.

Yiayia appears in the doorway with a tray. On it sits a large mixing bowl, a bottle of white wine vinegar, fabric scissors, cheesecloth, two kinds of tape—masking and Scotch—and a spiny aloe leaf. She comes toward me. Water sloshes. The dull scissors glint under the dimmed overhead light.

She gives the tray to Ben and says, "Ela, you're the nurse."

Yiayia eases down onto her knees to doctor me, and I cringe before she even lays her eyes on my arms. I flinch as Octavia pulls the tiny Greek book out of her cardigan pocket. I cringe as she walks across the room to Papou. Flinch as Ling Ling leans so far forward she's going to fall off the couch. Cringe as Ben's nervous hands rattle the operating tray. Cringe, flinch, cringe, flinch. I'm having a slow-motion seizure.

Papou cradles the book on the wide expanse of his palm.

"What is this you have?" Yiayia asks him. She cuts a strip of cheesecloth and dips it in the mixing bowl. She wrings out the water and dabs dried blood from my arm.

Papou extends his palm toward her. Yiayia regards the coverless miniature book.

Papou reaches under his sweater and removes a pair of drugstore glasses from his shirt pocket. He slips them on his nose, slides them to the exact right spot on the bridge. Settles into the Eames chair. Props his feet on the ottoman. Adjusts the lamp over his shoulder. Sets the brightness to the perfect setting.

Yiayia sighs with impatience. She's already cleaned the blood from my arms. The mixing bowl water is swirling with red. She cuts more cheesecloth and applies the vinegar. It's pure acid. I bite my lips to keep from screaming.

"Good girl," she says.

Since entering the study, Yiayia has not acknowledged

Ling Ling. She's kept her back to the bleach-blond bombshell: *a maybe or maybe not so nice surprise*. Me, I'm *poofu, poofu*. Yiayia predicted our fine mess: two girls in her grandson's scarves. If pressed, I'm not sure which one of us she'd choose for Nick. I doubt anyone is good enough. Maybe my endurance will better her opinion of me.

Papou opens his mouth to read from page one. He is proud of his education. His brows furrow as ancient Greek filters through his brain. Understanding comes letter by letter. He mouths the English equivalent before speaking aloud. But he doesn't say anything.

I can't read his lips. Digital time blinks by on the side table Bose stereo.

"Papou, what?" Nick asks.

Yiayia breaks the tip off the aloe leaf and squirts green gel along the outlines of my scratches where my skin is raw. She cuts more cheesecloth and tapes the rectangles directly to my arm. She blows cool air through the gauzy pores. She says to Papou, "Speak. Your grandson asked you a question."

Papou says, "Oh, Nick. Nico mou. Forgive me. I am so sorry. You have to believe your yiayia and I didn't know."

"Know what?" Panic creeps across Yiayia's face. "Sorry for what?" She waves for Nick to help her stand, grabs his hands, and hoists herself to her feet. She hugs him and then rears back to look at his face. She presses her hands to his cheeks, pulls down his lower lids and studies the whites of his eyes.

She plucks a hair from his head and rolls the root between her fingers. Nick looks scared. Yiayia screams at her husband, "Sorry for what? Tell me, you old fool! What have we done?"

Papou points at the little library book.

Yiayia rushes to him and hovers over his shoulder. She leans her body into the lamplight. "Oxi!" she cries as she reads. "No, no, no! I don't believe it! I *won't* believe it! Nico mou, where did you get such garbage?"

"I didn't get it. Mary got it."

"STUPID GIRL!" Yiayia's thunderous voice fills the room. "HOW COULD YOU BRING THESE LIES INTO OUR HOUSE?"

Tears hit me in the face like a water balloon. I cover my mouth to muzzle myself, but my skin stinks of vinegar. I gag. I'm not sure what's so bad about the Greek book, but by the way Yiayia glares at me, I know that the betrayal it reveals is much worse than my being a narc.

Nick says, "Yiayia, Mary didn't mean anything. She doesn't know what the book says. What does it say?"

"*Antidotos!*" Yiayia screams. "For *everything!* But *for you*, it's too late!"

Nick sinks to the floor right in front of me. He leans back against my socks and bare knees. He cups my ankles.

I can't believe it, I feel tingles—the good kind. In the midst of all this.

Papou raises his arms for calm. "Please! This book could be

caca. What's listed here: *Gorcones*, *Kerkopes*, *Orinthes*, *Styphalides*. Myths. I've never known any of this in real life." He looks over his reading glasses at his wife. "Have you?"

She says, "Oxi. But your theory is caca. Because we do not *know* does not mean it is not so. Until our Nick, we thought what he has is as pretend as the rest of this book. But our boy is real. That book, what it says, must be real too."

Nick says, "Tell me the antidote."

"Oxi, it's fiction."

"But Papou, what if it's not?" he pleads.

"If it is not, we have apologized. It is too late for you."

Nick's head drops. He is devastated. I place my hand on his shoulder.

Ben asks, "Is it too late for me and Mary?"

Papou whispers, "No."

Nick's head drops farther, to rest on his bent knees, but he reaches back and places his fingers on top of mine. I spread my fingers so he can slip his in between. Everyone is looking at us, but I am not shy. I understand Nick—always will. He's stuck. And I don't think being stuck with him is the worst place I can be. I know there are worse places. I've lived there. My sister has too. Damn it, I'll make sure Octavia is happy with me. I'll convince her not to tell our parents. I'll steer clear of Country Club and his strays. I'll stay away from Yoon's deli. I won't hunt. I'll figure out how to love. Nick and I will keep to ourselves. I won't let curiosity kill what we have.

Yiayia asks Ben and me, "You would leave Nico mou to suffer alone with what he is?"

I say, "I won't."

Yiayia's eyes soften in my direction. I am chosen. Ling Ling can suck it.

Papou says, "There's a cure for the new ones, we tell them." And then he reads: "*Ailouros prospopoiia. Ailouros*, meaning cat. *Prospopoiia* meaning personification, from *prospa*, meaning mask. *Antidotos*: To rid the body of this condition, the afflicted must drink the blood of a natural-born cat moments before it dies. Thus, you reject the species. The natural cat dies, so dies the cat inside you."

Nick says, "Papou, I can do it!"

"Oxi, let me finish. The book says the antidote is good only if you complete it before fully transforming a second time."

Yiayia says: "For you, Nick, it has been many times."

Papou says to me: "For you, it looks like your time is nearly up."

Orange fuzz sifts through and feathers out the gauze on my arms.

Ling Ling squeals: "I did it to her! I'm turning! It's happening to me!"

Nick laughs, but there is no humor in it. "Nothing's happening to you. Mary's arms are furring because of all the time you spent with those strays—petting them when they were turned. When you scratched her, you must have had their residue under your nails. Mary, you've got maybe an hour. You have to go."

"Where?"

"The Cellar."

"What's Mrs. Wrinkles going to tell me that she hasn't already?"

"She isn't going to tell you anything. You're going to kill her."

The room falls silent.

"Oh, shit," says Ben.

"I'm not going to kill that old cat," I tell Nick.

"Oh, yes, you are!" Octavia grabs my elbow and jerks me out of my chair.

I say, "But she's the Queen of the—"

"I know who Mrs. Wrinkles is, Fergie! She is a library treasure! A research miracle worker! The reason I'm the youngest Purser-Lilley debate captain ever! But that cat is the answer. Her chaperone is blind! What more do you want, a silver platter? You get in, you get out, it's over before you know it. You do this one awful thing and then we can all go back to normal."

"Except for Nico mou," says Yiayia.

Ben asks, "And what about me?"

"I'm sorry, sweetie," Octavia says. "Kill your own cat."

"Can't we both kill it?" he asks.

I say, "We are not killing Mrs. Wrinkles!"

"Seriously," Ben asks Papou, "what's the book say? Can Mary and I both drink from the same dying cat?"

Papou rereads what he translated. He squints at the text. "I do not see why not."

"What's wrong with us staying the way that we are?" I ask quietly.

Ben says, "Don't we have enough problems?"

"What problems? Debate team? Rope-climbing? Getting an A in Fem Lit? Finding someone who likes us *just the way we are*? These aren't problems. They're coming-of-age clichés! Ben, something amazing is happening to us. It's who we are. And it's who'll we be for such a very short time. It'll be over before we know it—probably before we can legally drink!"

Ben does the math. Three hundred and sixty-five days times five years plus a minimum of fifteen months of being blue in addition to being scrawny equals one hell of an awkward phase. Ben doesn't shave more than his upper lip yet. He gargles with Proactiv. The turning doesn't seem so short anymore. He confirms, "Five years is forever."

He runs out of the study and down five flights of stairs—from the sound of it, he takes two steps at a time.

Octavia screams at me, "Go after him! Don't let him get to her first!"

"I'm not killing Mrs. Wrinkles. Don't you get it? I'm not getting fixed!"

"You are, even if I have to drag you to The Cellar myself."

Nick nudges Octavia. The movement is sudden but smooth. He sidles into her. His arm brushes hers. His weight leans into her body and nearly knocks her off balance. He wanted her attention. He's got it. At first, it ain't good. I think Octavia's going to hit him harder than she slugged Ling Ling. But then he does it again: sidles into her with his whole self. Her angst mysteriously quells. Without a word, he's communicated that they're on the same side. She needs to calm down or they'll never get through to me.

Nick picks his scarf up off the floor. He steps forward, and I accept it from him. I touch my throat. A thin line of orange fur has circled my collarbone like a cheap gold necklace. The turning is coming over me so quickly, I don't feel the tingles—the good or bad kind.

Nick says, "Mary, if you don't fix yourself, this scarf will be all you'll have left of me. I'll never speak to you again."

Ling Ling perks up on the sofa behind him.

He senses her movement. He doesn't have to say what he's thinking. I know he'll say anything to keep me from fully transforming a second time. Nick hates the turning. He'll hate me for not trusting him that it's the worst way to live. He'll hate me for refusing an antidote that he would take in an instant if our positions were switched. If he has to, he'll tell me that he will be Ling Ling's boyfriend for real. If I ignore him, he'll do it. I'll spend the rest of my turn-time turning without him and be forced to see him with Ling Ling in class, between classes in the hallways, at my sister's debates, idle at the bus stop below my parents' bathroom window. Nick can smell me, so he'll follow me everywhere and drag Ling Ling along. I know it's true. I remember what he told me: cats are spiteful and never forgive.

I bolt.

My feet slip down the stairs in my speed. I hang on to the banister and swing my legs out as I leap to each landing. I knock pictures off walls. Glass shatters from frames. Religious icons tumble and clunk. An avalanche is after me. So is everybody else. I'm in the mudroom. Octavia, Nick, and Ling Ling are in with me too. I shove my feet into my loafers and throw on my coat. I fling open the front door. From somewhere behind me, Yiayia is crying. Smoke rolls out of the kitchen. The pastitsio has burned.

chapter twenty

In the basement of Webster Library, Miss Ryan stands before The Cellar door, barring unforeseen customers. She fumbles with her dangly earring. She looks to Octavia and then to me: Octavia's anonymous friend to whom something weird is happening. Miss Ryan knows what's weird about me. She knows what's happening in her used bookstore. When she speaks, I know she is speaking of Mrs. Wrinkles.

"My dears," she pleads, stepping aside to let the four of us stream in, "help her."

Octavia and Nick stay on my heels as I tear through the main room to the Old English graveyard. Ling Ling lags behind, slowed by the weight of her designer bag. Miss Gibbs waits for her to catch up and then ducks out, I assume to stand vigil with Miss Ryan. They think we are here to rescue their cat.

It hits me that after I get through with the sphynx, Octavia will never be able to show her face here again. The Cellar is everything to her. But she's forfeiting her secret haven to keep our family together. To keep my sister, I shouldn't hesitate to sacrifice the turning, something equally special to me. I shouldn't think twice about killing Mrs. Wrinkles if that's what Octavia wants.

Through the Old English bookcase that overlaps the entrance to the book well, I spy Yoon's Nantucket Reds and yellow dishwashing gloves. He purrs, "Hello, Kitty. We've been waiting for you. I knew you'd show up. Come see. The kid here has out-moused you."

Inside the well, Ben has Mrs. Wrinkles by the scruff of her neck. The sphynx is half in and half out of Mr. Charles's coat. She is stoic. Mr. Charles does not rise from his stool. He grips Ben's forearm. His long fingers are vines.

He says, "Young man, you do not want to do this."

Nick says, "Mary, get close. Be ready to drink her blood when Ben cuts her throat."

"Cuts her throat?" cries Ben. "With what?"

Yikes. I guess neither of us thought this through.

Mrs. Wrinkles coils her tail around her body and taps the top of Ben's bare wrist. There is a sizzling. An eraser-size circle of bone sears through his skin. The bone disappears behind a dot of silvery blue.

Yoon says, "Do it, kid. Kill her. Before it's too late."

The silvery blue dot branches out, scorches, and rings Ben's wrist like a handcuff. His face contorts as he looks to me for help. He doesn't want to go through this alone, but I'm not sure what I should do. Bite Mrs. Wrinkles? Disable Mr. Charles, a blind retired librarian? Ben's brow and upper lip drench in flop sweat. The sphynx's tail taps three of his fingernails. They all flip back and fall off. Sizzle, sizzle, sizzle. Tufts of silvery blue fur emerge.

Yoon encourages him: "Like swallowing a mouse, kid. Put her head in your mouth, and suck like a straw."

"Young man," Mr. Charles warns Ben, "if I feel your breath, I will kill you. I am not afraid of prison. I'm used to small cells and strange company. Don't try me."

Ben opens his mouth. His jaw quivers. He's in agony and he's scared and he's repulsed by what he's gotten himself into. He tilts his chin to his chest. Mr. Charles won't allow him to raise Mrs. Wrinkles to his mouth. Ben can't bring himself to bend over to her. He moans. His moan turns into yowl—a loud, long, mournful cat's cry.

"Do it," Yoon hisses.

"Why do you care, Yoon?" I demand. "What are you even doing here? I thought you wanted us to be like you. If Ben and I drink her blood, we go back to normal."

"You're not going anywhere, Kitty. And I'm not letting you near this old bag of cat bones. Your life as a turn is too good to throw away. You're special—even more special than me."

Nick says, "Shut up, dude."

"You haven't told her? Why wouldn't you tell her? You hate us that much?"

I say, "What are you talking about?"

"Nothing," says Nick. "Help Ben. He's having a panic attack."

Ben has stiffened. He still has hold of Mrs. Wrinkles, but his shirtsleeve is fattening as thick fur spreads from his wrist toward his shoulder.

Yoon coaxes him: "Go on, kid, use your free hand to bash her brains in. Crack that walnut! Once she's dead, you'll be free from all this. And Mary and I will—"

"Dude!" Nick interrupts.

Yoon protests, "It's her destiny."

I say, "What destiny? To be a turn-cat?"

"No, Kitty, to be so much more."

"Nick, tell me!"

Yoon purrs, "I'll tell you."

I say, "I want to hear it from Nick. I'm here because he convinced me to come. I'm about to kill a cat because Ben won't do it. I'm going to cut my own cat out of me because my sister won't live with me if I don't. And because…" Oh, hell, I'll just say it! "And because I want Nick and me to be together."

"Mary, I want that too," Nick says. "But if you don't fix yourself, your life won't just be ruined. It will be over. Country Club wasn't just up here sniffing around for territory. He was looking for you. He smelled you like we all can.

"Orange cats are genetically alphas. Orange females are genetically rare. Orange female turns are near-myth. There's never been one in the States. Not since the Turkish War has there been one in Greece."

Yoon adds, "In Korea, forget about it—it's been so long."

Nick says, "Mary, orange turns are *rulers*."

"My queen!" Yoon exclaims.

He actually drops to one knee. He places his gloved hands on either side of my feet and kisses my shoe. And then the other one! His lips are so strong, I feel their pressure through the patent leather. He looks up and blinks—his chestnuts turn to jewels. His emerald eyes tempt me. His incisors are long lumps behind his closed lips. I want him to open his mouth and let me touch their length and fine points. He smirks, but this smirk isn't smartass; it's knowing. Yoon knows there's a part of me that wants to find out if it's good to be the queen. There's so much I want to explore, but Nick and Octavia won't let me.

Yoon lifts and lowers his shoulders as if reading my mind. *Shrug it off,* he seems to be saying. *Don't let those scaredy-cats scare you.* I'm drawn to him. Say what you will about Yoon, but he's always been honest with me.

Nick, not so much. He lied to me about Ling Ling. He lied to me about Ben. He lied to me about me. True, he had an excuse for every lie—extortion, the right to privacy, my best interest—but he still lied. Saying nothing is the same as saying something untrue.

What else is Nick keeping from me? If I rule the doms, will Nick have to answer all my questions and do as I say?

Octavia and Ling Ling peer into the book well through

the shelves of the Old English overlapping bookcase. Ling Ling's cheeks are wet, but she doesn't make a sound. She doesn't want to call attention to her tears because she knows no one will pay her any mind in light of what's just been revealed.

Look at me! I want to cry. *Orange! Royalty! Near-myth Mary Richards!*

Octavia says, "Nothing's changed, Sheba. You still have to take your medicine. Yoon's using you. He wants your power. With you by his side, he thinks he's invincible."

"I am," Yoon hisses. "We are, Kitty! Ben, kill that cat!"

"Over my dead body," says Mr. Charles.

But it's Ben's own body that Ben is concerned with. Silvery blue fur creeps out of his shirt collar and covers one side of his face. His head looks like a half-molded peach. His eyes go gray. He shrinks by a foot. He crouches in pain. Mrs. Wrinkles hangs from his grip like a lantern.

Mr. Charles says, "Young man, give her here."

Ben does. Mrs. Wrinkles slips back inside her chaperone's lapel, and the pair easily make their escape because Ben is not a young man anymore. Poking his head out of his shirt sleeve, which now lies in a lump on the floor, Ben is a solid-blue powder puff. His gaping mouth is the size of a dime with tiny teeth like dime ridges.

He squeaks: "Mraw!"

Nick says, "See there, Ben lost his chance *just like that!*"

Snap! "You could turn *just like that!*" Snap! "We have to go after Mrs. Wrinkles."

Ling Ling glances over her shoulder toward the door through which Mr. Charles and Mrs. Wrinkles just vanished. She says, "Good luck."

Octavia says, "Mary, look at your arms!"

Orange fur pushes off Yiayia's bandaging. Bloody gauze dangles from slick strips of Scotch tape. I peel the clotted covering off both arms, slow and tortuously, the real way you peel off band-aids. Because, hello, here is this eerie calmness again. I'm not panicked. I am fascinated. I caress the fur, which feels like short strands of silk. I offer my arms to everyone. How can something so luxurious be bad?

Octavia won't come too near, but she and Ling Ling round the Old English bookcase and enter the well. I can see by Ling Ling's face that she wishes she were me. It is a new sensation to be envied. Exhilarating! Ling Ling pats my fur with two fingers, like I'm the baby book *Pat the Bunny.*

"Quit wasting time!" shouts Nick.

Yoon counters: "Let her do what she wants. You don't have to help her. Let me. Maybe, for once, somebody else knows what's best."

"Dude, you don't know jack!" Nick grabs hold of Yoon's yellow dishwashing cuffs. He jerks the gloves off. The gloves hit the floor with two sickening smacks.

Yoon stands stunned, as if he's been pantsed.

His hands (paws?) are as rubbery as the insides of his gloves and pasty black. There is no fur. No human hair. No cat claws. No nails. No fingernail beds. His digits (not *fingers* because there aren't enough joints) are bulbous, like charred marshmallows on broken campfire sticks. They're not threatening, unless you find deformity threatening.

Ling Ling makes a sound like she's going to throw up.

Yoon crosses his arms and tucks his hands between his biceps and ribs. They stick out behind him like runt wings.

Nick clutches my hands. He asks me, "This is who you trust to tell you what's best? Do you want what happened to Yoon to happen to you? Mary, the turning is not what you think it is. Please, believe me. We have to find you a pure-cat."

Octavia backs into a bookshelf and says, "A pure has found us."

"Mraw!" Ben squeaks. His blue kitten ears flatten as he and the rest of us bear witness to Country Club's gigantic, shadowy head crossing over the skylight.

Nick shouts, "Run!"

None of us do.

Nick and Yoon have to defend their turf. This is the domestic royal lair. They haven't been marred, so they're not officially strays. Despite Yoon's intention to take over the doms, I guess he'll have worse hell to pay if he flees. Ben too. Even if he runs, where can he go? He's teeny-tiny. If a book falls on him, he's a goner. Ling Ling scoops him up with one hand and slips him into the side pocket of her purse. She hikes it over her shoulder and stays put, just in case the Greek book, upon further inspection, lists a way for a girl like her to catch the turning.

The book well is darkened and chilled by Octavia's greatest fear, but she loves me. She won't leave me behind.

I won't leave my sister behind either. As Yoon predicted, I'm not going anywhere. I have family and friends and turf to protect.

Octavia was right: I am a hunter. The instinct is in me. X-ray me, the x-ray will be orange. This is MY choice: I want to kill Country Club.

He is a menace. He should be put down for what he did to the previous king. It wasn't a fair fight. And now he is here to fight me just as unfairly. As soon as I turn, I'll be no match for him. I'll be too small, nothing more than a mouthful. He'll kill me easily. Then I'll have no life, normal or not.

I have to kill him before I fully transform.

Country Club rears up and comes down full throttle. His front legs break the skylight. He plummets through shards of glass to land on my neck. His hind claws sink in to my shoulder blades, and his front claws dig into my scalp. I don't feel pain. I feel pressure. In an instant, I am flattened. My face is on the floor. Think of a five-pound bag of flour. Now, think of ten bags glued together; now, glue rusty nails to them and drop them on yourself from three stories up. This is what Country Club feels like: huge and solid and sharp and unforgiving.

Blood pours down my cheeks and pools beneath my nose. The blood bubbles as I breathe into it. It is a combination of mine and Country Club's from where the skylight tore his legs, belly, and face. What's not absorbed by his pristine white coat clots my hair.

My orange slingshot widens to fur my entire neck. Orange sprouts beneath my cardigan as Country Club shreds my back. He knows how to turn me, and he wants me to turn before I can defend myself.

The others hurl books at him. Country Club teeters on my spine. He hisses and chomps at the air to ward off helping hands. Fur burns through lines on my forehead where his claws connect with my skull.

I reach back and snare his mite-eaten ear. I twist it. A bit of that ear comes away in my hand.

Country Club scrambles off.

I spring to my feet.

But he's up, up, up, soaring from shelf to shelf. He spirals the book well, staining coverless books with blood. He leaves the rest of us in his wake, necks craned, spinning in place as we stare up after him.

Country Club settles on a shelf beneath the jagged skylight and studies me. He narrows his eyes, which are so blood-soaked that they look more olive than yellow. He licks blood from his nose, but his nose keeps on bleeding. Thick red drops fall and splatter our faces, shoulders, and arms. The tomcat is nonplussed. His chopped face is part of being the king. It is a punching bag daring me to hit it. He rocks, anxious for another aerial assault.

Fine, I think. I am ready to fight.

My cardigan is heavy with blood. I unbutton it, slip off one soaked sleeve and then the other.

Country Club bellows.

I bellow right back. My chest fills with fury, and I let that rage out. I don't sound like a girl. I don't sound like any cat I've ever heard. I like the way I sound. I am pure attitude.

Country Club plunges down the well like a white bowling ball.

I bag him with my sweater.

I don't know how I manage it. I wanted him; the King of the Strays is in my sweater.

I swing him against a hard oak shelf with all my might. *Thwack!* The sound is wet and bone-crunching. I've stunned him. Bagged, he barely fights. All his senses are cut off. His claws are pinned against his body. His weight is his only defense. My arms burn as I swing him over and over, rotating my hits against all four surrounding bookcases. The others duck. Blood sprays out of the sack over their heads and splatters my face.

"Enough!" Nick shouts.

When I drop Country Club, he doesn't fight to get out of his swaddling. Standing over him, the lump that is his body looks surprisingly smaller than he looked on the library roof; smaller than he felt on my neck. Nick peels away the cardigan to expose his front legs and belly. Country Club's back is broken in several places. Don't ask me how I know. I can tell just by looking at him.

Nick says, "He'll be dead in a minute, Mary. Drink."

Octavia says, "He's already dead."

Nick falls on the cat's unmoving chest and listens. He flicks a limp paw. He shakes him. "No!" Country Club's head lolls. "No! She has to drink *before* he dies!"

"Nick, stop!" Octavia says, "Let that dead cat alone. Look at her—she swallowed plenty!"

It's true. My school shirt is pasted to my body. I'm painted in Country Club's blood. My chin and lips are slick. I taste that coppery liquid on my tongue. It is in between my teeth, soaking into my gums. I can't believe my carelessness. I was so caught up in killing him, I forgot not to swallow what—as a result of killing him—wound up in my mouth. Any second now, the orange on my arms, back, throat, and forehead will petrify like pins and sink into my flesh. It's going to hurt so much. My eyes well up in anticipation. I tell myself I'll be fine. But I won't be fine.

I wail, "I didn't want to stop the turning!"

Blessedly, Nick can't stand it when half-girls/half-cats cry. He's not happy with my admission that I didn't want to get fixed, but he's happy that I fixed myself, whether I meant to or not. He wraps his arms around me. I'm shivering, awaiting the pain. He moves behind me and cradles me like he did on the twins' terrace lounge chair and the library handicap ramp. His arms align with mine. This time, he holds my hands.

Yoon looks disappointed, but he pecks my cheek. He wipes his mouth on his shirt collar. He presses his lips to my bloody cheek again. He is cleaning me. When my fur pierces my skin, he'll help me through it like he did the first time.

Ling Ling looks on, jealous but respectful. She holds her bag close and strokes Ben's kitten head.

Octavia frowns. The youngest captain ever of the Purser-Lilley debate team is struggling with what to say. And say something she must because she still won't come near me while I'm in this state.

Finally, Octavia breathes, "As soon as this is over, I'll make it up to you."

But my orange doesn't go anywhere.

I ask, "Why isn't the antidote working?"

Ling Ling says, "Country Club's blood was diluted with yours, so maybe it's slower to take effect like it was with what was under my nails."

"Mraw!"

Ben jumps from Ling Ling's purse. He tiptoes through a puddle of blood and props his paws on the tomcat's ribs that lie underneath the death shroud of my sweater. On his hind legs, he's tall enough to bite a cardigan button. He tugs the button, his back feet slipping and sliding in the goopy redness, which turns his blue feet purple. But he persists until the cardigan falls away to reveal Country Club's pelvis and hindquarters.

What's round and white and fuzzy all over? This dead tomcat has got them.

"Nuts," marvels Octavia.

Yoon looks shocked and then stricken. "Mary, this isn't Country Club."

Nick cries, "But drinking his blood still counts. A cat's a cat!"

No, not this one.

We know we've made a mistake when the dead cat's freshly marred ear turns human. The rest of him transforms finger by finger, limb by limb, until before us lies the naked, crooked corpse of a teenage boy.

Yoon says, "It's a Saddam!"

The fire ants attack. They spool my body and fill in the fur. Their bites sting like venom, but I give myself over to the turning. I'm shrinking. Down, down, down I go! Above me, I see so many faces, so many moons.

Nick says, "*Mary*, (fill in the blank with how they're going to get rid of the dead turn-cat's body). *Mary*, (fill in the blank with bullshit about how nobody will miss him because he's a runaway stray)." *Mary*, (I'll learn to live with remorse because war is part of being Queen)."

But it is Octavia who gathers me up off the floor. She raises me to eye level. Her look says: *What's happened has happened.*

Whatever our future, good or bad, she is with me. She

caresses my tiny body against her cheek. I curl up in the safety of her hands. Her voice gives me tingles. I am named.

She says, "Call her Kitty."

acknowledgments

Thank you to my editor, Dan Ehrenhaft, who lit a Sourcebooks Fire under my butt and gave me back my writing life.

Thank you to Susanna Einstein, who has always been an excellent advisor, but with this book also became my agent, proving that friendship and business can mix.

Thank you to Martin Wilson, who opened the door to YA and welcomed me in.

Thank you to Nina Delianides and Devi Rasaili, who reminded me that reading is supposed to be an escape.

Thank you to Vicki, Laura, Ellen, and Heather, who over a summer weekend at Myrtle Beach reminded me who I was at seventeen.

Thank you to Patti, Elizabeth, Laurie, Koula, and Joanie for never letting me go.

Thank you to the D.A. poker game for calling me Kitty.

Thank you to my parents, who, despite my failures, still tell me I can do anything. And to my sister, Elizabeth, who told me specifically that I could do this.

Thank you to my writing workshop of well over a decade: Ann Napolitano and Hannah Tinti, amazing authors and friends who always understand exactly what I am going through.

about the author

HELEN ELLIS is the acclaimed author of the novel *Eating the Cheshire Cat. The Turning: What Curiosity Kills* is her first young adult book and the first of a series. She lives in Manhattan with her muses Lex, Shoney, and Big Boy. She clings to her Southern accent like mayonnaise to white bread.